The Shipwrecked

T0162475

The Shipwrecked

*Contemporary Stories
by Women from Iran*

Edited by
FERESHTEH NOURAIE-SIMONE

Translated from Farsi by
Faridoun Farrokh and Sara Khalili

THE FEMINIST PRESS
AT THE CITY UNIVERSITY OF NEW YORK
NEW YORK CITY

Published in 2014 by the Feminist Press
at the City University of New York
The Graduate Center
365 Fifth Avenue, Suite 5406
New York, NY 10016

feministpress.org

Compilation and introduction copyright © 2014 by Fereshteh Nouraie-Simone

"The Shipwrecked" and "Dogs and Humans" translation copyright © 2014 by Sara Khalili

"Mermaid Café," "Unsettled, Unbound," "The Burnt Sound," "Intercession," "A Bloody Day of Ashura," "The Bathhouse," "The Wandering Cumulus Cloud," "Grammar," "The Queue," and "Tehran" translation copyright © 2014 by Faridoun Farrokh

"The Maid" is reprinted with permission from the Center for Middle Eastern Studies at the University of Texas at Austin.

All rights reserved.

 This book was made possible thanks to a grant from New York State Council on the Arts with the support of Governor Andrew Cuomo and the New York State Legislature.

No part of this book may be reproduced, used, or stored in any information retrieval system or transmitted in any form or by any means, electronic, mechanical, photocopying, recording, or otherwise, without prior written permission from the Feminist Press at the City University of New York, except in the case of brief quotations embodied in critical articles and reviews.

First printing December 2014

Cover design by Drew Stevens
Text design by Suki Boynton

Library of Congress Cataloging-in-Publication Data
The shipwrecked : contemporary stories by women from Iran /
edited by Fereshteh Nouraie-Simone ; translated from Farsi by Sara
Khalili and Faridoun Farrokh.
    pages cm
  ISBN 978-1-55861-868-8 (paperback)
  ISBN 978-1-55861-869-5 (ebook)
  1. Persian fiction—Women authors—Translations into English. 2.
Short stories, Persian—Translations into English. 3. Persian fic-
tion—21st century—Translations into English. 4. Women—Iran—
Fiction. I. Nouraie-Simone, Fereshteh, editor. II. Khalili, Sara, trans-
lator. III. Farrokh, Faridoun, translator.
  PK6449.E7S55 2015
  891'.5530108—dc23
                                                        2014032352

CONTENTS

INTRODUCTION

THE SHIPWRECKED IS a collection of short stories written by a generation of Iranian women writers whose works mostly emerged after the 1979 revolution. Thematically, the collection deals with gender and sociopolitical issues in contemporary Iran. The centrality of politics in everyday life, and changes wrought by revolution, war, and religiously imposed segregation are reflected in these stories. Politics play out on women's bodies, the personal becomes political, and the public sphere invades private space to silence dissent. The unifying thread linking the stories is the struggle for freedom, self-assertion, and subjectivity in a confined social environment.

The protagonists in the stories are not actively engaged in politics, nor are they protesting in public, but they are angry and disillusioned. They address the realities of their society with their voice to deconstruct the dominant power and to challenge notions about gender politics. They want individual freedom and a less intrusive political space. They have become skillful in the art of survival and in subverting the controlled public space. And they have carved out a place of their own in which they are free to think and dream.

To understand *The Shipwrecked*, it is necessary to understand the complicated history of the 1979 revolution, which was a turning point in Iranian history. Hoping for a better future, a wide range of political groups representing different classes and ideologies took part in the revolution to overthrow the Pahlavi monarchy. The secular groups had little in common with religious factions except the leadership of Ayatollah Khomeini, the charismatic religious figure with mass appeal, who provided a common purpose for a disparate coalition: to overthrow the monarchy. One salient feature of the revolution was the widespread participation of women fighting for social justice, human rights, and political freedom.

Soon after the revolution, secular and Islamist forces clashed over the direction of the country. The secular opposition was outmaneuvered and marginalized, and a hardline Islamist camp ascended. Khomeini, the founding father of the Islamic Republic, promoted a policy of rapid Islamization as the key to social change and political control.

The cultural policy of the regime was aimed at creating an Islamic identity by reshaping public space through gender segregation, the enforcement of strict Islamic dress code (including mandatory veiling), and monitoring of proper moral conduct. Most aspects of women's lives became subject to state intervention.

Ironically, the Islamization process and the gendered policy of the regime gave women, especially those from traditional families or low-income groups, the opportunity for social participation, higher education, and employment. In the process they gained gender awareness, political consciousness, and agency. Some of the writers represented here fall into this group.

The large scale contribution of women to overthrowing the old regime, participating in the Iran-Iraq War of the 1980s, and assuming an active role in civil society laid the groundwork for women to push the gender boundaries of Islamism in favor of women's rights and feminism.[1] The postrevolutionary period also brought the flourishing of literature written by women as a powerful medium of artistic expression, giving them an empowered public voice. Literary production became dominated by women, and a mass readership led to the publication of a record number of novels, short stories, and poetry.[2]

A younger generation of women writers, some of whom grew up in the postrevolutionary era, rejected the traditional narrative style in favor of exploring new non-linear and fragmented literary techniques. The format of

---

[1]Parvin Paidar, "Gender of Democracy: The Encounter between Feminism and Reformism in Contemporary Iran." *UN Research Institute for Social Development*, 29 (October 2001).

[2]Nazila Fathi, "Women Writing Novels Emerge as Stars in Iran," *New York Times*, June 29, 2005.

these works range from the narrative/anti narrative style to impressionism, to magic realism, and other experimental forms. The varied literary forms in *The Shipwrecked*, many of which employ allegories or metaphors to explore multiple meanings, work collectively to reveal the stresses and strains of social life, the detriment of censorship, and disillusionment with overtly religious ideology.

The protagonists, who are sometimes the narrators, deal with the everyday experience of women in public and private realms. At the point we find them in the stories, most are restricted in their movements, either literally or physically. Their confinement comes in the form of jail cells, their homes, and even clothing they must wear in public. They mistrust all authority, including parental authority. Some watch passively as events unfold before them, others try to gain control over their lives. Each story presents characters frustrated by daily pressures, harassment, or an uncertain future.

The loss and disillusionment which replaced the hope and exhilaration that followed the revolution is represented in the title story, "The Shipwrecked," by Moniru Ravanipour. Using allegorical gestures and magical realism, the narrative reveals what is hidden—the horror and violence citizens face in speaking up and for resisting authoritarianism. The story is an elegy to the death of freedom, and to the memory of those taken away. In a haunting, dreamlike narrative, a woman in a cold, dark cellar laments what has been lost and feels compelled to write. The magic grows out of the painful reality, and the flight of fancy lands on an unstable shore that pulls the dead and living into the depth of the sea, where only there are the silenced and drowned free to speak up and cry out for freedom.

In "The Maid," by Goli Taraghi, a privileged family is frightened and feels betrayed by the social upheaval the revolution brings. Their servants abandon them, demanding a share of the family's wealth. In an attempt to cling to a familiar lifestyle, the family hires a new maid who has a clouded past and who causes more anxiety and mistrust . The overarching theme of the story is the turmoil the revolution brought to a class-bound society and the lack of trust that now pervades it.

In "Mermaid Café," Mitra Eliyati describes the tension, anxiety, and fear a crowd experiences as it is easily manipulated into attacking a tavern and destroying it as a relic of the past. The story is told through the eyes of a young adolescent boy who is infatuated with the mermaid figure perched at the top of the door. In his eyes, the inanimate figure is transformed to flesh and blood when he catches a glimpse of a woman behind a curtain crossing herself. The story juxtaposes the youth's sincerity and honesty with the pretense of piety from a hypocritical crowd that frequents the tavern but is ready, in the name of public morality, to lie, cheat, and destroy.

"Dogs and Humans," by Fereshteh Molavi, is set against the chaotic backdrop of postrevolution, when fear and confusion dominate and shots are routinely heard. It depicts a period of social upheaval and rapid change. Drawing a parallel between a dog and her puppy and a woman and her sick child, the narrative style and complexity of the story resists a simple answer to how the characters have come to where they are and what their fates will be. Instead it acknowledges the contingent world they live in, where nothing can be taken for granted.

Sofia Mahmudi goes further with textual experimentation in "Grammar." The protagonist wryly ponders his life and his death posthumously as a study in grammar. His existence and the details of his demise are expressed through comparing them to parts of speech. Is the protagonist trying to gain control over his environment by searching for himself in confrontation with syntax?

In "The Burnt Sound," by Behnaz Alipour Gaskari, a young schoolgirl is imprisoned in solitary confinement for spray-painting political graffiti. She clings to every sound that comes through her prison wall. The heartfelt songs she hears from a garage next to the prison inhabit her cell and become her constant companion. She fantasizes about the young apprentice, whom she has never seen. She hears the daily shouting, and the abusive vulgar language of the shop owner and his street-smart roughnecks. The boy is obviously being harassed and possibly sexually abused. He stops singing his sweet, melancholy songs and takes drastic action. Did he do it out of revenge or desperation? Has he finally tragically escaped from his own prison in the process?

Corporality and violence are interlinked in the "The Bathhouse," by Shahla Zarlaki. It is set during the Iran-Iraq war at the time of air raids, when Iraqi bombs were dropping all over Iranian cities and neighborhoods. Women's bodies are violated when a bomb explodes near the bathhouse, sending the women into chaos and darkness. The sound of the explosion may have caused the miscarriage of a pregnant woman, who has collapsed on the bathhouse floor. The violence of war becomes a reality in flesh and blood that defines the violated body.

In "The Queue," by Shiva Arastouie, the protagonist has been denied her degree for some unexplained reason. She is instructed to go to a certain office to obtain it. Now married, she has been cloistered in her home, and the act of trying to retrieve her degree forces her to confront her sheltered existence in contrast with her years as a student, when she was capable and independent.Ultimately, after standing for hours in a queue, and exhausted from waiting a whole day in the heat and noise of a crowded street, she is turned away without her degree as the office closes. She returns home defeated only to once again be forced to observe her life—this time from the outside.

In Zohreh Hakimi's story, "The Wandering Cumulus Cloud," a married daughter who is subjected to domestic abuse pushes back against the dominant tradition of the paternalistic laws, asking for divorce and seeking to expose the oppressive gender order. Her father's primary concern is the family honor, the scandal a divorce would present, and the disruption of social order. She is told to be a dutiful wife and accept her lot, or to be a slut who embarrasses the family and is unwelcomed in the parents' home. The father urges her to go home, and "just be patient for a while."

"Intercession," by Mitra Davar, incorporates echoes of the religious festival of Ashura and its rituals into the everyday life experience. The age-old pageantry, sacrificial slaughter of animals, and self-flagellation of the ceremony mingle with the protagonist's memories of a lost love and her reflection on her marriage and children. The story portrays a belief system, with all its superstition and sacrifices, told to be capable of performing miracles and relieving hardship and misfortune. In reality it is a potent tool of persuasion, of conviction, and of political hegemony. As the protagonist muses, the dead "seem to be with us for ever and ever."

"A Bloody Day of Ashura," by Masih Alinejad, captures the frenzy and anxiety of a political demonstration that ends in violent confrontation with the security police. A group of activists joins a protest march, mindful of state violence and security police. When a member of the militia on the side of the security police is injured in the process of trying to provoke the crowd to violence, a member of the group steps forward to protect him and quells the growing violence of the crowd.

In Moniru Ravanipour's story, "Tehran," the themes of change, loss of trust, and betrayal are played out against the cityscape. The city—full of luxury goods, choked in traffic, and bared of its tree-lined streets—becomes the site of transition from hope to despair that followed the short-lived halcyon days of the revolution. The city becomes a repository of varying values and experiences, and a metaphor for hypocrisy, deceit, and corruption.

The protagonist in "Unsettled, Unbound," by Fariba Vafi, finds there is no place to hide from the watchful eyes of her inquisitive landlord. The intrusion that invades her privacy leaves her no moment of rest. The only remedy is to leave the abode that once held the promise of peace, tranquility, and relief from the chaos outside. Better to be unsettled and free than to be constantly under the watchful eyes of an intruder. She challenges the sexist, patriarchal assumptions of the culture by giving up the comfort of the place in order to be free, to move at will, and to define a new life for herself.

The collection of short stories presented here provides a glimpse into the cultural and social currents of contemporary Iran and gives us a small sample of the rich literature produced by Iranian women in the postrevolutionary era. In spite of all the sociopolitical problems, economic hardship, censorship, and prohibition from publishing, an impressive number of Iranian women from diverse backgrounds have achieved great literary success and recognition. Their writing, from a variety of perspectives and experiences, broadens the literary discourse. The emergence of feminism and sociopolitical awareness has enabled female writers to challenge the sexist and patriarchal assumptions of the culture, to break down traditional gender barriers and, through each writer's distinct literary voice, to transform consciousness and experience.

—Fereshteh Nouraie-Simone

The Shipwrecked

Moniru Ravanipour

SHE CONSIDERED WRITING, "the woman was sitting in the cellar." But she had never seen the cellar. She had to write, "the woman was in the hallway" or someplace dank and salt stained, "with the blistering cold of the island and the winds of December." Then she remembered that the island isn't so cold in December and it is in early January that the weather takes a breath and is rid of the heat and humidity. She had to write, "January, and four lit candles in that small dark room or cellar," which must have been wet, because wherever you are on the island, if you dig even a few inches into the ground, water will seep out. Grandmother, who is buried in this old cemetery, always said, "Here everything floats on water, everything. We're just fooling ourselves thinking we live on solid ground." Grandmother was right, there is no dry ground on the island, and it's worse in a cellar. Its floor must be wet. There are cracks in the ceiling and the walls are salt stained.

She could write, "the woman was alone with a wet wooden bed and a blanket in which someone was wrapped."

And the blanket was new, checkered pink and white. At times like these they usually take the best things and then the pink-and-white blanket gets muddied. Dirt and mud stick to it and bloodstains slowly spread on it resembling a crab reaching out its claws beseechingly in every direction. A crab, a crab that wants to escape, escape in every direction. A crab that has lost its mind, that reaches out its claws in every direction yet remains in one place. In one place, on the checkered blanket, and only its claws stretch out and reach the edge of the blanket, the blanket that will surely get muddied or stained with a mix of blood and mud if Golestani is not tied to something, to a tree, for instance. Afterward Golestani must have fallen: first his knees buckled, he tried to remain on his feet, but the next hail of bullets mowed him down like a storm that uproots a tree, and then sparrow-like, he shuddered and a pair of hands untied him. And still bent over, Golestani slid to the ground headfirst, and then those hands took hold of his feet and dragged him. Dragged him to the side so that they could tie the next person to the tree. A tree that smelled of gunpowder, that had long smelled of gunpowder. But what tree, what massive tree is there at the harbor that can withstand this? A palm tree certainly can't: with the first person and the first barrage of bullets it will be done for, and a silk-tasseled acacia will never let you tie someone to its trunk and kill him. Ten days before she died, Grandmother saw with her own eyes the silk-tasseled acacia tree that had been pulled up by its roots from a town square, wailing like a grieving woman and heading toward the sea to drown itself.

It was never revealed who shot the seagull, but in a mournful arc it had flown off the silk-tasseled tree and Grandmother said a drop of its blood must have fallen on the tree.

She got up. She didn't want to think about Grandmother and the memories that never left her. She must write the story, the story of the cellar, and not think about anything, not about Grandmother, not about the silk-tasseled tree, and not about the island's palm trees that have been sapped of their strength. No, they didn't tie him to a palm tree. A palm tree couldn't endure it, even if it was its first time. No, there are other ways. For example, they could have hit him on the head, rendered him unconscious, and then tied his hands behind him and stretched him out on the ground facing the sky and shot him straight in the heart. If they did shoot him in the heart, there would have been no need for a final bullet in the head, surely there would have been no need . . .

Mrs. Golestani hardly said anything. She was dazed and dumbfounded. Mrs. Golestani's chopped words were of no use. But it is as clear as daylight that a man like Golestani wouldn't easily let them tie his arms and legs and pin him down on the ground. He must have struggled and thrashed about, and then they struck him on the head, and this, this shows that there must be mud on the blanket.

She picked up a cigarette. Outside the window the sky was black and the wind was spiraling in the palm trees. The wind's strange, ominous howl! It was near and far, and something, something was rippling before her eyes. Just like when the breeze blew over Grandmother's silk *minaar*, Grandmother's green lace headscarf.

The cigarette had unraveled. Bits of tobacco were dangling in front of her. She walked up to the window. She heard the rustlings; it seemed a group of people were secretly, fearfully emptying the coffins. It seemed out there in the dark, people with shovels were throwing dirt in the graves. It seemed everything was still continuing, all the things that had started six months after Grandmother's death. "Come on Friday nights," Grandmother had said. "During the week the dead go to the sea. It's not good to recite the prayer for the dead over empty graves."

Terrified, she looked at the calendar on the table. She was relieved. It was Monday night. All the dead from the cemetery were now in the sea, even those after Mr. Golestani had been buried by night. Now, none of the dead were in their place. The dead only slept in their own graves on Friday nights, and during the week they were in the sea, in the depths of green waters, someplace where they could have open discussions without fear and foreboding and speak their minds and shout as much as they wanted. Now the island was safe and the dark was not frightening and she could peacefully write her story. Without being afraid of Mr. Golestani and without being afraid that in the dark his slim, long hands will suddenly grab onto the window ledge and he will climb up and look at the sheets of paper and say, "Girl, this isn't the time for such nonsense." And she will answer, "Oh, Mr. Golestani, not everyone has to think like you . . ."

Now it was Monday and the cemetery wasn't terrifying. The sea filling up with corpses one night or one day and the island emptying of life, the dead, tired of putrefying deep in the waters, pooling their anger and returning to dry earth . . . no, these tales were not for now. The island was still full of living people and she could peacefully write and ignore Grandmother's superstitions. She just had to focus on the story and fill the sheet of paper that was still blank.

Well, the woman was sitting in the cellar . . . in what state could she be at this moment? The night before they were on their way back from a party, and the woman had told it like this: "I was looking in my handbag for the key when two people emerged from the dark and said, 'Mr. Golestani, if it isn't too much trouble, we have a simple question,' and they took him away."

She had heard this from Mrs. Golestani late one night after the incident when she had gone to Golestani's house. She couldn't ask for details about the two young men. Mrs. Golestani had even forgotten what they looked like. But still, she could come up with something. For instance, she could describe them as having their hands in their pockets, with their collars turned up against the chill and the cold winds of February, leaning against the wall, waiting.

She had tried to get Mrs. Golestani, with her eyes wide with surprise and her thin lips closed tight, to open up and talk, but it was useless.

The following day, just like the first time they came without warning and took Golestani away, Mrs. Golestani bought a few kilos of fruits and took several sets of clothes and a pink-and-white checkered blanket and went there; she must have been hopeful and anxious. And the moment when they told her? Mrs. Golestani's hands remained up in the air, holding the clothes and the bag of fruits. Like a statue she stood facing the young man who had spoken those words. She probably couldn't see anyone and if the young man wasn't accustomed to this, he must have run off, or perhaps he stayed there, smirking at Mrs. Golestani's frozen hands and the oranges that one after the other fell out of the bag and rolled onto the floor . . . Mr. Golestani didn't like apples, otherwise the young man could have picked up one of the apples rolling on the floor and taken a bite. And then someone screamed, a woman who didn't know where she was, who she was, or what she was doing, and then there was the rented pickup truck and Mr. Golestani whose head wobbled on the woman's lap and the rough and uneven road that seemed to have been intentionally littered with rocks so that no one could reach the cemetery easily . . . so that the pickup truck bounced around so much that Mrs. Golestani had to hold Golestani, wrapped in the blanket, tight in her arms so that he wouldn't tumble out of the pickup truck.

And then it was dusk and everywhere was closed, even the cemetery . . .

Mrs. Golestani said, "I wouldn't have taken him there even if it was open. I wanted to see if it was true. I wanted to unwrap the blanket and wake him up so that he would come and finish hanging the curtains. The hammer and the curtain rods were still on the floor and on the mantle, and Golestani . . . Golestani . . ."

Remembering Mrs. Golestani crying troubled her. She was crying so hard. It was a crying that had no cure and like a painful wound could disturb the cellar's mournful air.

On the face of a woman sitting beside a blanket, a blanket in which Golestani's body is wrapped, and four candle flames that cast shadow and light in the cellar, there must only be perplexity and confusion, not tears that one cannot describe in words. Words that seem to be mocking you. Just like Mr. Golestani who always teased, "So you're again writing in that notebook. My dear girl, you have to become a historian. You have the indifference and dispassion of history writers."

Regardless of anything Mr. Golestani said, a writer has to pursue everything, everything from the beginning, when someone comes and says, "If it isn't too much trouble, just a simple question . . ."

And now the sea was full of dead people who went

away with this same simple question and their feet never touched dry land again.

The wind had become stronger. The rustle of the palm trees, drifting weeds and twigs and commotion filled the air. A strange and vague commotion. Nervous and frightened whispers.

In front of her, the window opened onto darkness. The salty smell of the sea wafted into the room. Everything was damp and sticky. There was light in the window of Golestani's house. A grieving, despondent light, a yellow light that seemed to have died years ago, stretched as far as the window's edge.

She lit another cigarette and stared out at the blackness of the palm trees that blanketed the graveyard.

There were only three women. Three women and the others, who stood at a distance and with their finger on a gravestone, found some excuse to watch. Mrs. Golestani was sitting next to the checkered blanket. Dazed, she was gazing at the earth and the sky. It was obvious that she felt stifled by the world. Terribly stifled. And she, clad in a chador, with her notebook in her handbag and her finger on a stranger's grave, was sitting there, watching.

When the gravedigger came, he leaned on his shovel and with his dirt-covered fingers flipped through the three sheets of paper Mrs. Golestani gave him and shook his head. The grave was ready and all he had to do was slide Mr. Golestani into it and cover him with dirt. They had the public prosecutor's permission, too. But the gravedigger said, "I can't just bury whoever shows up." And then he glanced over at Mr. Golestani's Adidas shoes and heaved a sigh.

From where she was sitting, she saw the gravedigger take a five hundred-tuman bill from one of the women accompanying Mrs. Golestani and then he sat at Golestani's feet and yanked the shoes off his feet and untied the shoelaces with his teeth. Golestani had no control over his legs; they just lay there like a pair of dry sticks. And finally the gravedigger stood up, holding a pair of Adidas shoes. The grave was now ready. . .

"Grave ready, Adidas shoes," she tried to write these words on the top margin of the page, above the word "Monday." The paper was wet, the pen was streaking, and the ink was discolored, as if it had remained unused for years.

Her head ached, her mouth tasted bitter, and the pack of cigarettes was on the table, cigarettes that with the slightest touch would unravel. Mr. Golestani was a smoker. All the dead who have now gathered beneath the sea waters and are talking with each other or sitting alone in a corner and trying to heal their bullet wounds with sea plants or the remains of dead oysters were smokers.

She picked up the pen to write, and she wrote, "The smell of mustiness, the smell of decay, and the flames of four candles reflecting on the cellar's salt-stained walls and the shadows and light they created. The woman was sitting at the head of the bed, with her elbows resting on the bedframe and her lips moving. The blanket had slipped off his face and Mr. Golestani, pale and drained of blood, was lying there. His mouth was open. Half-open with his teeth exposed, as if he had wanted to laugh heartily but had swallowed his laughter, and Mrs. Golestani was a thin and pallid apparition."

When she looked at the page, she saw that it only bore the grooves made by the tip of the pen and that the wet paper was still white. Surprised, she got up. How fortunate that Mr. Golestani, with those black eyes and the gleam that always shined in them whenever she saw him, wasn't there to wag his long, slim finger and say: "You're kidding yourself. You pretend you want to write, yet you run away from face-to-face encounters. All alone, writing to what end? History can only put someone on trial when the accused either no longer exists or has lost his power . . ."

She felt as if someone was beating drums in her head; she had difficulty breathing. She was standing in front of the window. There was no light anywhere. She glanced at her watch that was rusted. With her long brittle nails she tried to scrape away some of the rust. The watch face had a yellowish hue, the hands had stopped on two. Just like the hands on Mr. Golestani's watch that had stopped on three and the date that remained on Tuesday, December 26. "They shot him at three o'clock, in the middle of the night," Mrs. Golestani said. "Watches stop working the instant they shoot you."

And now it was two o'clock in the middle of the night

and there was a faint light coming from over there, from the direction of the house, Golestani's house . . . No, the light wasn't from the cellar, it was from a window, which someone had perhaps intentionally half opened, so that while standing there, facing the darkness, she could look directly ahead and count the graves, graves that stood in rows, one after the other, small and large, as far as infinity.

If Mr. Golestani were alive, he would now be sitting at that window reading a book. He would read and leave the window half open, but Mr. Golestani is dead and his wife is probably sitting at that window, crying. The same crying that is impossible to include in the cellar story.

The wind suddenly slammed the two window panes shut. She was frightened. Of that vague commotion and that noise which sounded as if people, young people, in the depths of the green sea were pushing away the water with their crippled hands so that they could go from one side to another. She was frightened. She searched for her grandmother's voice. The voice was old and far away; the dead only stay in their place on Friday nights. On other nights, they are in the sea. And then a voice nearby, closer and more familiar, her mother's voice consoling her so that she would not be afraid of anything. "There is still a long time left before the island empties, empties of residents. It is then that the dead will return to their homes and lives and settle down here. . ."

Why should she be afraid? It must be Monday, and they were in the depths of the green waters, chatting and confiding in each other. No one could hear them above the water, whatever they said, whatever they wrote, but Monday . . . Monday of what year was it? She stared into the darkness and listened. It sounded as if someone was struggling to climb up to the window. She looked. A pair of hands, thin and long and wrinkled from having been underwater for years, and then she saw Mr. Golestani who pulled himself up to his neck into the window frame.

"You're still thinking about the cellar?"

Disappointed, she looked at him and realized that Mr. Golestani had again come to say, "You are here, deep in the green waters, like the rest of us . . . you have been here for a long time, you must accept it."

MONIRU RAVANIPOUR is one of the most prominent writers of postrevolutionary Iran. She is the author of several distinguished novels, including *Heart of Steel*, *Gypsy by Fire*, and *The Drowned*. Her collections of short stories, *Kanizu* and *Satan's Stone*, were translated and published in the United States. A former Brown University fellow at the International Writers Project, Ravanipour now lives in Las Vegas and is affiliated with the Black Mountain Institute at the University of Nevada.

The Maid

Goli Taraghi

WHEN THE REVOLUTIONS CAME, those who worked for us simply got up and left, even Hassan Agha, the cook, who had been with us some forty odd years, and his wife, Zahra Khanum, who always swore we were the apple of her eye, and Morteza the Gardener, who at each prayer heartily blessed Father and everyone in the family—and even Nanny Karaji, who had grown old in our household and was an integral part of it.

With the departure of the old cook, a part of our family history was wiped out—all those memories that involved him: Friday family luncheons, New Year's charity dinners, the pleasing mix of aromas wafting from jars of tomato paste and preserves and condiments in the upstairs pantry, the soothing jangle of dishes and pots and pans, the magical taste of home-cooked meals, and the seemingly unassailable security of the kitchen. With him and Nanny Karaji leaving us, the Shah skipping the country, the uncles hastily migrating to far-off corners of the world, a neighbor's house being confiscated, and Shamsolmuk

Khanum being accidentally "martyred," a door was being closed forever on our past. It was the end of an era and the beginning of something new, something ambiguous, vague, unfamiliar. The logic of daily events escaped us, and history, like the onslaught of a foreign horde, swept away old customs and pillaged what was left with an assortment of unmatched pieces that did not fall into any recognizable patterns.

Hassan Agha disappeared suddenly and surreptitiously—no goodbyes, no reasons or excuses for leaving. We thought he had been taken ill or—God forbid—had died in one of the clashes of the revolution. We could not imagine that he had left of his own volition until his sons turned up as local revolutionary-committee[1] henchmen and began sending threatening messages. Zahra Khanum, too shy and diffident for a face-to-face encounter, sent an emissary to let us know of the complaint she was filing against us with the authorities.

We could hardly believe any of this. We should talk to Hassan Agha, we decided. Mother and I got dressed and headed for his residence. Nobody answered the door, although we could hear someone inside and see a pair of eyes watching us from behind a curtain in a window. Embarrassed and humiliated, we turned back. In the alley

---

[1] These so called committees were created in the course of the revolution to orchestrate demonstrations in urban neighborhoods against the former regime. Later, they were unofficially in charge of enforcing civil laws and Islamic standards of social conduct.

we ran into Morteza the gardener, who turned his head and did not acknowledge us.

We were alone and helpless in a cold and spiritless house. During the power outages at night, we sat around the oil lamp and held our breath in fear anytime there was a knock on the door. The younger ones in the family were planning to leave, heading out for Europe, but were concerned about the older folks who would not hear of leaving, nor could they be left behind to fend for themselves. Grandparents, though decrepit and handicapped, had no intention of dying anytime soon. Parents, younger but unwilling to migrate and change their lifestyle, dreaded loneliness, revolution, and war. Uncle Colonel was already on the lam, and his mother could not sleep at night, fearing imminent famine and looting. Auntie Malak was afraid of the Afghan wetbacks and was sure they would cut her head off. She would pass a trembling finger across her double-chinned throat, as if feeling the sharpness of the knife in her plump flesh. She would moan in agony of fear. My physician uncle, surpassing all in wisdom, got himself a pair of grown German shepherds (which immediately proceeded to bite Mother on the thigh and my aunt on the ankle), installed several alarms and an early warning system, and hired a security guard to watch him and the house.

Mother was hurt mostly by Hassan Agha's desertion. She never mentioned his name but could not forget him either. She insisted on hiring a new servant mostly to assuage her wounded pride. But how could we bring a stranger into the house? How would we trust a stranger in this day and age? I was planning to leave, and war was about to break out. I had to find a trustworthy person to care for Mother. Mohammad Agha, the neighborhood carpenter, had a reputation for being a solid and decent man. We had known him for twenty years and had learned to count on him. He was different from the others. I broached the matter with him when he was in the house changing the locks. I told him I was looking for a smart and trustworthy person to look after my mother, and the reason I was talking to him was that my brother the engineer trusted his judgment and had good things to say about him. I was almost certain he would not be interested, finding excuses to deflect the rapprochement. Surprisingly though, he jumped at the suggestion. "With pleasure," he said, as he put down his saw. "I am beholden to your family and the engineer. His wish is my command."

I could not believe it. People promise things but never carry through. I looked at him doubtfully. "Do you know someone trustworthy?" I asked. "I mean, like yourself?"

"Do you think I would recommend an unsuitable person to the service of the Grand Lady?" he said, somewhat miffed. "These days," he continued, "one is suspicious of one's own shadow. I had heard about Hassan Agha and was embarrassed by his behavior. Sincerely, I could not look the engineer in the eye. What a world this has turned out to be! Even a dog does not recognize his master. But we are obligated to you and the Grand Lady's kindnesses. Believe me, my mother blesses the engineer every night at prayer. If she finds out that the Grand Lady needs help, she would volunteer herself."

I thought he was buttering me up. Mohammad Agha, an observant man, read the look of skepticism on my face and took up the issue directly. "I will go right now to my aunt's house," he said resolutely, "and, with her permission, fetch her daughter to attend the pleasure of the Grand Lady."

This was ideal, exactly the person we had in mind. It did not matter whether she could cook, sew, or keep house. The important thing was that she was Mohammad Agha's cousin, and thus, reliable. She would alleviate Mother's concerns and introduce some degree of order in our disrupted lives.

Mohammad Agha explained that his cousin had never worked anywhere and was mostly a homebody, shy and withdrawn, religious and chaste. In other words, she was exactly the person we were looking for. I was only afraid that her mother might oppose the deal. As an added incentive, I let Mohammad Agha know that there would be something in it for him. He rejected the idea with a vehement shake of his head and waving of his hand, which left me somewhat mortified for thinking along those lines.

Mohammad Agha left his mission, and I rushed home to bring the good news to Mother. Nothing could top this.

At the house, I did not see Hassan Agha himself, but

his wife and the bevy of his brood were there, lined up in the corridor near the entrance. Zahra Khanum, trying to be inconspicuous, was standing behind the sons. She held her head down, and the black chador covered half her face. The sons were nervous and ill at ease, mumbling incoherently. It was the son-in-law who was in control of the mission. We did not know him well, but he certainly was in command.

They wanted money—half the house, part of the garden. Somehow, they knew that legally and in practical terms they had not a leg to stand on, so every time Mother cast ferocious glances in their direction or made a biting remark, they blushed and retreated. There was only one thing certain: neither side was in the same position as in the old days. Shy and maladroit, Zahra Khanum took it up herself to point this out. From where she stood, she jutted her head and squealed in her high-pitched voice, "So why was there a revolution?" Good question, we all thought.

Going directly to the heart of the matter, my brother asked, "How much do you want?" This took the men by surprise and made them even more inarticulate. Zahra Khanum, holding a corner of the chador in her teeth, batted her trachoma-damaged eyelids uncontrollably. The son-in-law, less mindful of us, blurted out a figure, which in his view was exorbitant. For us, however, it was less than expected. We agreed and the meeting ended abruptly.

The anticipated arrival of a new maid and Mohammad Agha's agency in the matter seemed to soften the blow we had just suffered. "To spite Hassan Agha," Mother intoned, "I will give this girl a higher salary; I'll give her the upstairs room; I'll personally find her a suitable husband. . ." I interrupted her and urged her to hold off her munificence until later. But she was excited and on a roll: "The old, stupid, ungrateful jackass. When he came to us he had not even done his national service and did not have a penny to his name. He arrived barefoot from Arak,[2] and I sent him to adult literacy classes. When he brought his diseased, trachoma-stricken cousin from the village, I spent so much on her medical bills that I even paid for his children's schooling. I put together a dowry richer than my own for his daughter's wedding. Now they have the gall to ask, 'What was the revolution for?'"

An hour later Mohammad Agha arrived with his cousin. She was young and fresh faced, rather plump but in a pleasant way. She was wearing a chintz chador but no stockings. Mohammad Agha saw me stare at her bare legs and said quickly, "Forgive her impromper appearance. I just picked her up and brought her over. My aunt was not home. She was going to put on black stockings, but I was afraid it might take too long. So I told her to get going."

"We are not strangers anymore," said Mother, "but I wish she'd come with the approval of her mother."

"In fact," rejoined Mohammad Agha expansively, "*you* are Zeynab's mother. We are all your servants."

---

[2] An agricultural region in central Iran.

Zeynab lifted her head and stared quizzically at Mother. She then chuckled, returning her gaze to the floor.

"If memory serves, my son had always spoken highly of your aunt. She is a respectable lady."

I knew Mother had never met the woman, but she was so excited that she had convinced herself of the truth of her statement, convinced that the aunt was exactly the kind of person she expected her to be.

We sat on the veranda, and Mother, in a convivial mood, struck up a conversation with Mohammad Agha, asking about his family and making complimentary comments about his wife (although she had never set eyes on her). It looked like she was trying to delay negotiations about Zeynab, relishing the pleasure of the moment, like a tasty morsel of food in her mouth. She steered the conversation to the inflationary spiral of prices, shortages of water and electricity, my brother's run-in with the authorities and his recent incarceration, the theft of Uncle Doc's car, and Hassan Agha's traitorous defection. If the conversation continued along these lines, I decided, it would lead to some sensitive issues. So I interrupted her and asked Mohammad Agha to tell us about Zeynab.

"Sit down, dear girl," said Mother. "You'll get tired standing up. Think of this as your own home and of me as your own mother." She then stood up, walked to the fruit basket, piled a plate with fruit, and offered it to Mohammad Agha. Zeynab, who had been standing all this time, sat on a chair at Mother's insistence.

"This girl has never worked anywhere," said Mohammad Agha. "She is exceedingly naive and simple. My aunt too is old-fashioned and religious. She has made this girl into a true homebody."

"That is how it should be," declared Mother, eying Zeynab with approval. Zeynab dropped her head down and gave a childlike, meaningless giggle, every inch an ingénue, inexperienced with the ways of the world.

"As a matter of fact," Mohammad Agha continued solemnly, "the parents of this poor child died in a car crash when she was barely two months old. She herself was tossed out of the car window, and it was only by divine providence that she was spared. My aunt, devout and godly as she is, raised this child as if her own. She is the apple of her eye!"

Mother, casting a pitiful eye in her direction, announced, "I will personally watch over her . . . find her a husband. They could live in the cottage at the end of the garden. The husband could work in my son's office. If they had children that proved studious, I'd pay for their education . . . send them abroad."

An agreement was reached soon, and Mohammad Agha, in something of a hurry, rushed out of the house. But before he left, he made two firm provisos: Zeynab was not allowed to leave the house under any circumstances— on her days off, the aunt would come for her—and she was not to make or take phone calls.

Mother nodded vigorously in agreement. "Yes, of

course," she said, "all these restrictions are absolutely necessary, what with this girl being so young and pretty. You may trust her with me."

Zeynab put away her bundle and took off her chador. "I'll begin from here," she declared, as she cast her glance around the kitchen. She then grabbed a broom, opened the windows, piled the chairs on the table, and began to sweep.

"There you are," I told Mother. "That's a maid for you!"

"What a gem!" replied Mother, ecstatically. She immediately remembered Mohammad Agha's injunctions and told Zeynab that first she should say her mid-day prayers. Zeynab was fully engrossed in her work, beads of perspiration forming on her brow, the thin fabric of her dress sticking to her pale skin, outlining her young firm flesh. She ignored Mother's bidding, mumbling something about work being more important. This thrilled Mother. Even my suggestion that we should first eat something fell upon deaf ears.

By now Zeynab had moved the cupboards, the refrigerator, and other kitchen furniture, and was cleaning the space behind them.

"This is what I call an immaculate, sensible person!" Mother proclaimed. "The important thing is to clean everything, even what is not visible. That filthy Zahra Khanum only passed a hand over things and let it go at that." Mother was now fuming. "And that good-for-nothing husband of hers, Hassan Agha, just eating and sleeping and maligning. Good riddance! To hell with them!"

Zeynab's dress was deemed short and too open at the neck. We decided to get her a smock and thick hoses. Mother suggested that she wear a light headscarf when we had company. At this suggestion, Zeynab cast an amused glance at us and gave a laugh, which struck me as incommensurate with her look of shy innocence. We postponed lunch until she finished cleaning up the kitchen.

"It is cleaning the nooks and crannies that counts," said Mother. "See how everything shines! This girl is a godsend, an angel. I will take care of her myself—find her a husband, set her up in the lodge at the end of the garden, and have her children sent to America. And if her husband knows something about driving and gardening, he will be the chauffeur and gardener. Forget about the ungrateful Morteza—filing a complaint against us. Imagine! One hair on this girl's head is worth a hundred like that scumbag."

All in all, Zeynab was too good to be true, and with this realization came a certain amount of concern. "Makes me sick to think she may not stay," said Mother, her face etched with worry. "She is young and gullible. Neighbors will get her away from us. We are finished if your Auntie Malak finds out about her. Mustn't praise her a lot. With such shortage of good help, she'll be whisked away in no time."

A knock on the door brought our hearts to our mouths.

It was Mohammad Agha. "Miss, he is here to take you home, I guess," I suggested to Zeynab. "To hell with him," she blurted out, with one hand at her hip, glowering at the doorway. "Still a free country, isn't it?"

Mother cast a surprised and confused glance in my direction. The bewilderment in her look shot through me. There was something grating and strident in Zeynab's voice that ran counter to her diffident, peasantlike smile.

It so happened that Mohammad Agha had come to collect his tools. We asked him to stay for lunch but he declined. He was in a hurry to get somewhere. Before he left, though, he took Zeynab aside and talked to her under his breath. Like an impetuous, playful child, Zeynab shifted from foot to foot, scratched her upper thigh, and rolled her eyes with impatience.

"The more advice she gets, the better," noted Mother. "There is good reason to be concerned." No sooner had Mohammad Agha left than Zeynab returned to her cleaning zealously, as if her life depended on it. Despite her small stature, she was amazingly strong, easily moving heavy furniture around. "Dear girl," pleaded Mother apprehensively, "don't move that antique vase, please. It might shatter. No need to dust the china. Please leave the crystal chandelier alone." It was no use. Stubbornly, Zeynab proceeded with her taste, ignoring Mother's pleas. Eventually we gave up and left her to her own devices. Although she insisted on total obedience from the household staff, Mother watched Zeynab with obvious satisfaction as she went though the house bestowing a sheen of cleanliness on everything she touched.

She finished around two in the afternoon. Not feeling hungry, she pushed her food aside and drank a whole bottle of water. She then washed her face and wetted her hair in the sink, plumped down in the middle of the living room floor, and went out like a light. Perspiration oozed from her pores, and an animal warmth radiated from her young, firm, healthy flesh. The short skirt was riding up her thighs, revealing a glimpse of her flowered underwear. She looked younger in her sleep, with her pink cheeks and turned-up eyelashes. Something primitive and amorphous in her body coupled with that impish, sensual smile, imbuing her childlike presence with ambiguity and suggestiveness.

In the early evening the telephone rang. It was Mohammad Agha's aunt who wanted to talk to Mother about Zeynab. I listened to the conversation from the extension in my bedroom. The woman sounded more literate and cultured than expected from a peasant. She said she worked in an office, knew of our family, and had a nodding acquaintance with my father whom she admired. Getting to know my mother would be a great honor, she added. She had also heard good things about my brother and me, and believed Zeynab to be exceptionally lucky to have ended up in our household. She mentioned, sort of offhand, that Zeynab had many suitors, and it was possible that some of them might try to talk her into marriage, something she would not allow, nor would she allow her to talk to any men.

Profusely, Mother assured her that Zeynab's virtue would be protected at all costs and, at the proper time, she would herself find her a suitable husband, send her children to school, etc. Reassured, the woman hung up and we all felt that we now had a reliable housemaid on a permanent basis. I even fantasized about taking trips, certain that Mother was securely ensconced in her home with adequate help. My brother, too, would rest at ease, once he heard the good news, thanking God for this piece of good fortune.

The dusk had barely fallen when Auntie Malak arrived at our house. Her eyes popped at the sight of Zeynab. "Where did this come from?" she exclaimed. Mother tried to shrug it off. She said casually that the girl was a relative of Mohammad Agha, the carpenter, that she was not much good and completely untrustworthy. The last epithet shook up Auntie. "She is not Afghani, is she?" she asked apprehensively. Mother hunched her shoulders, shook her head, and curled the corners of her mouth as a gesture of uncertainty. "What? Are you crazy?" Auntie exploded, raising her hand to her throat. "If she is Afghani, you're gonna be done with tonight! How stupid! Where did you get her, anyway?"

Mother was being obnoxious, of course, while I was trying to calm Auntie down. But she wasn't to be comforted, casting suspicious glances at Zeynab. "I'd rather die a death of loneliness, wash floors, and clean house by myself than let a stranger into my life," she announced. "Just the night before last they raided the home of an elderly couple and cut their heads off. That's what the paper said. It is the work of Afghanis, they say. Same thing with Mrs. Khavary. They gagged her in her kitchen and beat her on the head with a club. They tie up the kids and twist their necks like chickens."

Zeynab brought in the tea tray. Mother looked at her pridefully and said, "Zeynab is every inch a lady, and I am happy with her." As she picked up the empty glasses, Zeynab turned and looked at Mother with a grin and murmured, "Don't count your chickens before they're hatched!"

I couldn't believe my ears. Mother gave a hollow laugh, trying to look as if she hadn't heard it. But Auntie, on full alert, heard everything and let her jaw drop. "Did you hear that? Don't count your chickens . . . What gall, the little bitch!" she exclaimed.

Desperate for a way out, Mother groped for words. She said dismissively, "Ah, you blow things out of proportion, Auntie. She just said something. Not that she has any education. Perhaps she just wanted to be complimentary. The end is always better than the beginning."

Auntie was not to be comforted. She was worried, most of all for my brother. "What if she reports on us?" she speculated.

Mother, frustrated and irritable, gulped down her tea.

"So what? We haven't done anything. What have we to be afraid of? We have nothing to hide," she said firmly.

At this point, Auntie rose to her feet and straightened the large scarf covering her head, pulling it almost down to her eyes. "You must protect yourself," she advised. "Just the fact that you're sitting here hale and hearty is itself a crime. Our crime is that we still have our heads on our shoulders. What's worse?"

When Auntie departed, Mother and I felt ill at ease. We began reading the afternoon papers with a bad taste in our mouths because of Auntie's blabbering. Mother stood up, looking around indecisively, as if she wanted to say something but had changed her mind. She sat down again.

By this time Zeynab had finished her work. She sidled toward me, craning to see the pictures in the paper. "These are all dead?" she asked.

"Let me see," interrupted Mother, "have you recited your evening prayers? Mohammad Agha was very particular about that, you know." Ignoring her, Zeynab pointed to the paper. "What's written in there?" she asked, her curiosity piqued. When the telephone rang, she jumped. "I'm sure it is for me!" she chirped, as she reached for it. Mother blocked her advance, yelling "Wait a minute, girl!" as she picked up the receiver. "Hello, hello," she repeated into the phone, but there was no answer.

"I told you it was for me," said Zeynab defiantly. Mother, trying to control her temper, replied, slowly and deliberately, "You must never pick up the phone. Your aunt insists on it. Do you understand?" There was so much authority in her voice that even I was transfixed. Zeynab, pale and intimidated, gathered herself and lowered her eyes. "I'm going to water the flowers," she said timidly. But then she turned to me, and like an excited child talking to a playmate, asked, pointing to the newspaper, "What's written here? Are they dead? Must have been smugglers, right?" Without waiting for an answer, she careened down the stairs, picked up the garden hose, and turned on the tap. She took off her slippers, splashing water on her feet. She exuded the freshness of a flower patch, and her youth, like the fragrance of acacia vine, permeated the yard. She was childlike in her joyousness, making it hard not to excuse her occasional odd behavior and words. Mother was once again well disposed, forgetting the Auntie's injunctions. Her face glowed with a halo of satisfaction as she peeled an apple and shared it with me.

Our neighbor's servant, we noticed, was standing on the roof. "Look at that son of a bitch," Mother noticed, "ogling at my girl."

"Hey mister," she whooped, "what are you standing there for, feasting your eyes? Don't you know you can't invade folks' privacy? Get down or I am calling the Committee right now." The man snickered and shrugged his shoulders. "It is your own fault—your gallivanting in the yard unveiled. If you had any modesty you'd cover yourselves," he said.

"Can't we breathe free in our own house?" Mother wanted to know. She picked up her tea glass and turned to Zeynab. "Come on in, missy," she said. "From now on, don't get out there without a head cover."

I felt drained and listless. Without a word I picked up my books and newspaper and went inside. Zeynab squatted next to me, mumbling. Suddenly she said, "I just want to talk."

I ignored what she said and continued reading. She said again, "I know I am not supposed to talk, but I really want to talk."

"All right, go ahead and talk," Mother said impatiently. "What do you want to talk about?"

"I'm scared Mohammad Agha will cut my head off."

"You get up and get ready for your prayers. Don't think bad thoughts," commanded Mother. "Mohammad Agha is harmless," she said.

Zeynab got quiet and thoughtful. It was obvious she was dealing with some kind of an internal conflict. Absentmindedly, Mother was thumbing through the pages of a magazine when the telephone rang again but stopped before we picked it up. Standing motionless, Zeynab raised her hand to her face to hide an amused sneer. I looked at her, an ominous feeling going through me. Her behavior was certainly bizarre. She noticed I was staring at her. "What are you reading?" she asked, taking her hand off her face.

I held the book in front of her and asked, "How many

grades have you finished?" Mother, not waiting for an answer, interjected, "My girl, I can put you in adult literacy classes, if you want. Mohammad Agha said you have finished elementary school."

"I have a question," said Zeynab, changing the subject. "You are all so educated and understand everything so well. Just tell me how it is possible for two grown people to die in a car crash but an infant gets thrown out through the windshield without a scratch."

Mother and I exchanged glances. Deep in my heart I had a sense that trouble was ahead. Mother frowned with a certain look in her eyes. She pursed her lips, and deep lines appeared in the corners of her mouth.

"You are so naive," Zeynab persisted. "I'll be skinned alive if Mohammad Agha finds out I have opened my mouth. But you are so nice; I can't lie to you."

The doorbell rang. It was the sanitation man calling for a spot of lunch and his monthly allowance. We were left alone again after his departure. I pulled Zeynab aside and told her that talk like that disturbs Mother. "But I swear on the Koran I am not lying," she protested. "This woman who claims to be Mohammad Agha's aunt is lying. I don't know who my parents are. For all I know I may be a foundling."

As she turned toward us, Mother heard the last sentence. Color drained from her face. "Do you realize," she said sternly, "that if you lie, all your prayers will be nullified?" Zeynab laughed pejoratively. "Oh, come on, who says I pray? Mohammad Agha's aunt has never said a prayer in her life, and he himself is a drunk with no religion!"

Mother was almost in shock. "Look here," she warned, "I'm going to call her and tell her what you're saying behind her back."

"I don't care," said Zeynab, pouting. "She'll come and get me and throw me in the arms of strangers again."

We were speechless. The illusion of good fortune had turned into a receding cloud of dust. Transfixed, Mother and I stared at each other, lost for words. Zeynab, on the other hand, was excited by her boldness, knowing she was treading on forbidden ground. "I shouldn't have said that," she moaned, tears welling up in her eyes. "You are such decent people. I bet you'll kick me out now. Right?" she asked, whimpering.

The phone rang and I lunged for it. A woman's voice I couldn't recognize asked for Zeynab. "Who are you?" I queried.

"I am her mother and have just arrived from Ghazvin."

"But madam," I said curtly, "she says her mother has died in a car crash."

"Oh, she's not all there, you know, and says things," the voice explained. "I'll be there to pick her up."

Mother, with her ear pressed against the receiver, wondered, apprehensively, "Who are these people? Where did they get our phone number and address?"

"They are after me," Zeynab said "all those thieves and smugglers." If Auntie Malak had heard this, she would have fainted on the spot, I thought. Mother, too, looked pale, making me think that we were now in a real crisis.

"Do you know what you are talking about?" I snapped at Zeynab. "We have known Mohammad Agha for twenty years."

All this time, Zeynab kept glancing at me pleadingly, seemingly apprehensive of Mother and the misery that lay in her future. Words, as if churned by a force stronger than her will, poured out uncontrollably. Mother, vacillating and nervous, muttered, "Didn't I say we shouldn't hire anyone? Didn't I say we shouldn't trust anyone? How do we know what Mohammad Agha does in his spare time? He does only carpentry work here. We are not with him all the time. Who could have imagined Hassan Agha and that wife of his leaving us in a lurch after fifty years? Do you remember how she put her hands on her hips and stood in my face yelling, 'Then what's the revolution for?'"

This was a delicate subject and had to be changed. I turned to Zeynab and asked if she could honestly tell us who she is and how she got to know Mohammad Agha. We all drifted into the kitchen, which looked meticulously clean after Zeynab had finished with it. Impressed, once more Mother changed her tone. "Listen to me, girl," she addressed Zeynab, "don't be afraid and tell me the truth."

"I swear on the Holy Koran, I'm telling the truth." Zeynab asserted. "Until a few years ago," she went on, "I was in an orphanage. Then I was adopted by a rich engineer, Mr. Sham-Akhtar, and his wife. Three years ago she died. Mr. Sham-Akhtar married me off and moved lock, stock, and barrel to America. Turns out my husband was a heroin-smuggling gang leader, him and his mother and brothers. They tried to get me hooked too, but I ran away and went to the Committee and gave them their names. The guards came and took them all away. A little later, I saw their pictures in the paper, and the report said that they'd hanged my husband and two of his brothers. That made me happy. Then this woman who says she's raised me took me to her house and that's where I saw Moham-mad Agha. His job was to bring in girls. One night they sent a customer to my room, and I got into a fight with him. I cracked his skull with a flowerpot and ran into the street yelling and screaming. He was so afraid the Com-mittee would find out. That's how I ended up here. And now you are going to kick me out, I know."

I was in a real quandary. Was she sincere? I could not tell. I wanted so desperately to see through her. I pulled Mother aside. "We absolutely must protect her," I whis-pered, "if she is honest. We must change her life."

"Are you crazy?" Mother retorted. "It's dangerous. Didn't you hear? Heroin smugglers! She's sent her hus-band to the gallows. His comrades are not going to let go. They'll be after us. What if she'd tell the Committee all sorts of lies about us? I shouldn't have trusted Mohammad Agha. I never liked him much. Come to think of it, he does look like a cutthroat. That stupid and bad-tempered Hassan Agha! He was worth his weight in gold, compared to these folks. Fifty years he lived with us under one roof and not a pin got lost or misplaced, though he had control of everything in this house. What do we do now?" Mother said with a note of desperation in her voice. "I'm gonna call Mohammad Agha to come and get this girl out of here."

I felt it contingent upon me to show some backbone. "No way!" I protested. "First we must get to the bottom of what she says. If she is telling the truth, we can't hand her over to those wolves."

Mother was reluctant. "What if she is in cahoots with those thieves?" she said, now in the throes of doubt. Trying to defuse the tension, I told her jokingly she was worse than Auntie Malak. It suddenly occurred to Mother that Zeynab had taken a shower in the downstairs bathroom and had possibly seen the crates of wine bottles left with us by a friend for safekeeping. "Those crates are behind the bathroom window in the backyard," she said fearfully. "I am sure she has them! Now she has an advantage over us. One word and she'll report us to the Committee. Imagine that! Here we are, our maid's captive!"

"We'd better not talk about the crates," I said dismissively. "I'll dispose of them tonight somehow."

"Throw them in an empty lot or something," she suggested. "To hell with that wine. I told you not to store them in the house."

Zeynab, oblivious to us, was mumbling to herself absentmindedly and incoherently. "I had a good time in the engineer's house," she said to no one in particular. "Until his wife died and he went crazy. He'd cry every night and beat his head against door and walls and then turn on me and give me a good thrashing." She then reached for an apple and started gnawing at it, quiet and pensive.

That night we had an invitation to dinner at Mr. K's home, and this added to our ordeal. We were torn between suspicion and sympathy. For a moment, allowing sentiment to take over, Mother said, "Poor girl, snatched up by these wolves! We can rescue her. I'll keep her here . . . find her husband . . ." she muttered, her voice trailing off.

Before anything else, we had to do something about the wine crates, regardless of what we did with Zeynab. By now, we had thrown away all unsanctioned objects, such as playing cards, backgammon boards, videos, music tapes, incriminating photos, etc., all in fear of a raid. Mother covered her head even when she answered the phone. We kept the windows shuttered, went to bed early, and turned off all lights. We had cut down on socializing—which had taken a toll on Mother's temper. She was already demoralized by Hassan Agha's departure and Morteza's grievance lodged with the authorities. After a couple of short visits to Europe, Mother had toyed with the idea of liquidating everything and moving to the other corner of the world to get away from all this. But she had decided against it. How would it be possible to go into exile at her age to a land where streets evoked no memories and language was a barrier? How could one sit next to a small window all day and watch the never-ending European rain? Despite everything—the murderous Afghani wetbacks, religious-police raids, runaway inflation, Hassan Agha's desertion, war, bombardment, and insecurity—Tehran was home, and every part of it interlaced with her life. Even its problems and heartbreaks were meaningful and could be shared widely. Its rare moments of relief, too, were of a public nature. Death itself had familiar rituals, and life in this town, with all its chaos and agony, had familiar and comforting patterns for Mother and was latent with the expectation of better things to come. Living abroad, however, would have meant nostalgia for the past and recycling old memories.

Time was now of the essence and we had to take some action. Mother had the urge to do something drastic, something untoward, to protect Zeynab, this helpless creature, but was scared of the consequences. She was more inherently cautious than to act on impulse. That made her so much more desperate for a reasonable escape route.

"Did you notice how casually she spoke of her husband's execution?" noted Mother. "She almost sounded jolly. It made my blood curdle. I don't even know these people. But when I see their pictures in the paper and read the caption they have been executed, I get sick. But this girl sounds as if she is used to such things. She could do the same thing with us." At this point it looked like we had to get rid of her. But how? And how to deal with Mohammad Agha?

"I know you don't want me," said Zeynab, as if reading our thoughts instinctively. "I should have kept my trap shut. I know it was stupid of me to talk. I'm not going back to Mohammad Agha and that bitchy aunt of his. I just got myself out of their clutches. I know where I'll go."

"Where?" asked Mother expectantly.

"Back to the engineer, Mr. Sham-Akhtar," replied Zeynab with authority.

"But you said his wife is dead and he is in Europe," exclaimed Mother, thinking she had caught her in a lie. But Zeynab was right on the ball and came back with an answer. "But his mother is here and she liked me. Besides, I heard that he is now back," she came back without missing a beat.

The dry and hollow timbre of Zeynab's voice told me that she was lying. But to Mother this was a ray of hope. "That's my girl," she whooped. "You just do that. If they kept you all those years, they must be better than anyone else. You just go to their house, and I'll put Mohammad Agha and his aunt in their place for good."

"But you don't know that woman," warned Zeynab. "A few months ago she had some problem with a neighbor, and she told a bunch of lies to the Committee. They came and took that woman away."

Once more the color drained out of Mother's face. She immediately regretted pitching herself against the aunt. "Very well," she said, in retraction of her threat, "I won't get tangled up with that woman. That is none of my business. As for you, dear girl, just go to Mr. Akhtar's and stay there."

It was hard for her to utter these words but they had to be said. We had to extricate ourselves from Zeynab and her predicament. After all that had happened, we had to act conservatively, with self-preservation in mind.

As for the dinner party, it was decided that Zeynab should go with us. Mother helped her put on one of her old-fashioned winter garments with a high collar. When Zeynab saw herself in the mirror, she burst out laughing, almost like a child.

"I look just like the aunt, one of those madams," she said as she guffawed.

Mother winced. "Now you look respectable," she said defensively. "What was it you were wearing before? It was shameful."

While Zeynab was busy adjusting her outfit, I called a friend about moving the crates of wine. I knew Mr. K would take exception to having a stranger in his house, but we had no choice. We even thought of declining the invitation. But then we felt we needed the company. Besides, the affair was a farewell party for me in anticipation of my upcoming trip out of the country.

Mr. K did not easily let anybody in his house. He had made elaborate arrangements with trusted friends and relatives for coded ringing of the doorbell. He would alert his dogs to stand guard before he opened the door. The dogs had been especially trained to be suspicious of the chador and to attack women wearing it.

When we arrived, we touched the door and a light came on at the top of the doorway. When we rang the doorbell, we could hear a siren sounding inside the house, setting off the dogs. A metallic voice in the intercom asked, "Who are you?" Then another voice from behind the door asked the same question for confirmation. Following a long pause, the door opened and we entered. We hastily took off the chadors and other headgear before the dogs reached us. Mr. K immediately stared at Zeynab, who was putting away her chador. He then looked quizzically at Mother. I intervened and explained that she was not a stranger but a new maid we could not leave at home because we didn't trust her that much. I hastened to point out that we were letting her go the next day anyway. This not only failed to calm Mr. K, but exacerbated his agitation to such an extent that I began to regret coming to the party at all. Earlier that morning, sixteen people had been executed for an assortment of charges, including corrupt practices and infractions of religious moral standards. This had put everyone on edge.

Mr. K asked us to wait out in the garden until he had warned his family and guests of the presence of a stranger in the house. Zeynab was certainly proving a disruptive factor among us. We were all related, close-knit and like-minded. That night a foreign element had infiltrated our gathering, causing concern and discomfiture. Mr. K's wife, adjusting her headgear, sidled up to Mother, wanting to know why she had trusted a stranger. Bringing Zeynab had definitely been a mistake, but it was too late.

Zeynab, oblivious to the disturbance her presence had caused, was delighted to be at an affair of that kind. With wide-eyed curiosity, she was looking everyone over. At some distance from where the guests had congregated, a chair was placed for her with a bowl of fruit and confectionaries at her feet. Soon it was time to tune in to the Persian broadcast from Radio Israel. My Uncle Doc was addicted to foreign broadcasts and knew the wavelengths and schedules of all of them. But Mr. K cast a wary glance at Zeynab and signaled to him not to turn on the radio.

Auntie Malak wanted to know what Zeynab's wages were. I noticed that Mother was not averse to the idea of palming Zeynab off on Auntie. Accordingly, she began giving a praising account of Zeynab's housekeeping virtues. She hinted that the girl needed a home and did not expect any pay. The only reason why we were trying to place her was that we were leaving town for an extended period. The thought of an unpaid domestic excited Auntie, but she was too nervous about strangers to fall for it.

The party was not like always. Mr. K, given to telling tired old jokes, was now silent. Auntie Malak, who loved to discuss the news and current affairs, was wordless and pensive. So was my uncle, who had been told not to turn on the radio. The younger folks, usually garrulous and strident, were quiet and sullen. Tooba Khanum's husband, always critical and ranting about the sorry state of affairs, seemed on the verge of an explosion, now that Mr. K had whispered in his ear, pointing to Zeynab, to keep his mouth shut.

At one point, when Zeynab got up to go to the bathroom, the whole company simultaneously converged on Mother with questions. She held up her hand. "Listen," she almost yelled. "The girl is Mohammad Agha's niece, for goodness' sake. And you all know *him*. She is no stranger!"

Except for Mr. K, this was enough to set everyone's mind at ease. Even my uncle turned his radio on almost immediately. But Mother, always inclined to melodrama and wanting to share her anxieties with as wide an audience as possible, could not resist mentioning her uncertainties about Mohammad Agha's character. God only knows, she went on, but Zeynab had mentioned something about his involvement with heroin-smuggling gangs. She then dropped a bombshell: Zeynab had informed on her husband, resulting in his execution by the authorities. At this point Auntie Malak gave a loud squeal, raising her hand to her throat. "Afghani, she is an Afghani, I knew it," she croaked through choking sounds. "I'm outta here," she said, turning to Mother. "So you wanted to pass this one on to me! How could you? Did you want to have me murdered? You can't trust anyone anymore, not even your own relatives!"

Mother appeared puzzled and looked at the others questioningly. Mr. K, in extreme distress, looked at Mother and babbled, "These things are dangerous! Your son has just been released from prison. Just the mention of the word 'opium' these days is enough to send you to the gallows."

"We shouldn't have brought the girl," said Mother somberly. "Let's go."

Now that the party was in disarray, no one objected to our departure. We called Zeynab, who was playing with some children in the hall and watching television, looking so harmless and vulnerable. I wanted so badly to believe that she was sincere and that I should take her under my wing against the dictates of common sense. But that was beyond me; I did not have the willpower. When we got home, Zeynab was still in a buzz from the party and said nothing about leaving. She jumped in the bed she had spread in the downstairs hall and was asleep within minutes.

We had a rough night. In a state of high nervousness, Mother jumped at every sound. Early in the morning we were startled when the telephone rang. It was Zeynab's so-called aunt calling to talk to her. Mother spoke to her, calm and collected, explaining that we could not keep Zeynab because we were leaving for Europe. Sensing something was amiss, the aunt spoke diffidently. "I'm embarrassed," she said. "I should have told you the truth. This girl is a bit on the crazy side. Her father died some years ago, and her mother, my younger sister, lives in

Ghazvin and is a mental patient. I have raised this girl and I know she takes after her mother. She comes up with strange tales. Her mother arrived in Tehran yesterday and is dying to see her. I apologize for inconveniencing you. I'll just come and get her."

"Not so fast," replied Mother. "Let me talk to her first to see what she says." Mother did not wait for a reply and hung up.

The aunt had sounded reasonable and credible enough for Mother to change her mind once more. "We shouldn't have judged Mohammad Agha so fast," she said thoughtfully. "He's worked for us twenty years and has always been sensible and level-headed. This girl is lying through her teeth, confusing us in the middle of all this chaos. Of course we can't keep her if she is a mental case."

Zeynab, who has been eavesdropping behind the door, burst into the room. "I am not waiting for Mohammad Agha and his gang to come and get me. I'm leaving right now," she said in a rage.

"Where are you gonna go? Back to the engineer?" I asked. "What engineer?" she spat back. She then looked at me morosely, as if she was going to continue, but the fluttering of a moth behind the windowpane caught her attention. She remained motionless for a moment before she came to herself and hurriedly put on her shoes and chador. Before we had time to react, she left the house, slamming the door behind her.

"Oh my God, what do we tell Mohammad Agha?" said Mother, whimpering. "She was kind of entrusted to us."

For a while after Zeynab's departure, we were chafed with pangs of conscience. But soon a sense of relief came over us, now that the interlude was seemingly over. We were no longer involved. It was out of our hands. "Some people never change," said Mother, more in justification of our course of action than as a usual observation. "We tried to be charitable and give her a helping hand, and look what a commotion she caused! Good riddance! Never mind that we don't have any household help anymore." On this note we indulged in a moment or two of self-pity laced with an appropriate amount of sympathy for Zeynab and her kind, before putting the bizarre affair out of our minds and getting back to our normal routine.

Then came the first phone call of the day. It was Auntie Malak expressing her chagrin and disapprobation about our role in the events of the night before. For our part, we called Mr. K to tell him that the affair was over and he could relax. The doorbell rang just as we sat down for lunch. "It's Mohammad Agha," said Mother, considerably alarmed. She wanted me to answer the door and advised me that I deal with him firmly. I had no stomach for the encounter and felt a tinge of embarrassment.

Gingerly, I opened the door and was astonished by what I saw. There she was, Zeynab, perched on a motorcycle behind a dour-looking young man with a full, dark beard. Apparently delighted to see me, she jumped off the bike and rushed to the door. The young man averted his glance and stared at the ground, hinting that my head was not covered. "Excuse me a minute," I said, running back into the house to get my headgear. Mother followed me back to the door, panting. "Is she back? Has she blabbered to the Committee? What trouble are we in now?"

When Mother appeared at the door, the young man greeted her respectfully. "Dear lady," he said, "this girl is a distant relative of ours. Her father was a close associate of mine, God rest his soul, and we have known her family a long time."

"According to her, though," replied Mother, somewhat sarcastically, "she's all alone in this world. We've been told a hundred different versions. How come she's found family and friends now?" The young man ignored the remark and proceeded to produce an identity card, which he held in front of Mother's face. "I am an employee of Ghods Department Store and this is my ID," he said assertively. "This young lady is my brother's fiancée. My brother was in the war front and took shrapnel in the back, which paralyzed him. We ask that you look after her for a while until we know what's going to happen to my brother. It is not right that you let her roam the streets."

Zeynab furtively whispered in my ear, "He is lying. He is from the Committee."

We were in a terrible bind now. If that was true, we had no choice but to do his bidding. Before he roared off on his bike, he told us emphatically that we were not to turn her over to anyone else. We would be responsible if something happened to her.

Back to square one, we thought. Zeynab was elated,

like a dog reunited with its owner. She threw off her chador and hung around my neck, kissing me on the cheek repeatedly. She then picked up the broom and started cleaning feverishly. "A ball of fire she is!" exclaimed Mother, unable to contain her delight with Zeynab's work. "I only wish she weren't off her rocker. Now that she has reported us to the Committee, we have no choice but to keep her for the time being."

Auntie Malak was coming to lunch, and we were at a loss at what to tell her. A word about the Committee and she would have a heart attack. Mr. K would certainly sever relations with us altogether. So we called Auntie and postponed the lunch to another day, making some excuse. Meanwhile, Zeynab continued the work, humming under her breath, and occasionally stopping to chuckle for no reason at all. When she finished, she announced that she wanted to take a shower. This triggered the anxiety over the wine crates in the backyard. I went hurtling down the stairs to see if they had been taken away—and they hadn't been. Frustrated, I ran upstairs and told Zeynab to hold off on the shower. I signaled Mother to keep an eye on her while I hid the crates in the utility room. "What the hell," said Mother impatiently. "Dump that filth down the toilet and throw away the bottles in an empty lot."

The wine did not belong to us but it was proving to be a serious liability to keep in the house. As Zeynab started on her lunch, I emptied the wine, stuffed the bottles in a sack, and threw them in the trunk of the car. I drove all the way to Gharb Township, where friends of ours were having construction done, and flung the sack in a deserted corner of the lot. When I got back, Zeynab had finished lunch and was stretched out on her mattress fast asleep. There was a glow on her face, making her look sated, safe, and cheery. And I felt depressed. I was developing an affection for her, and that made me feel conflicted and at odds with myself. Every time she prevaricated or made up a new cock-and-bull story, she looked prettier and more appealing, eyes glinting and cheeks blushing, as if the risk of being caught in a lie added to her attractiveness.

The doorbell rang. It was Mohammad Agha. He walked in quietly, looking somber and demure. He was his usual self—noble and dignified, inspiring trust. What a monster we had made of him! It was Zeynab who had ensnared us in her web of insane lies.

Deferentially, Mother invited him to take a seat and offered him tea. I turned to Zeynab and said that she should get packed and go with him. She grabbed my arm and drew me away, as she whimpered, eyes streaming, "I swear on the Koran, I swear to God, this man is worse than Shemr. He has ruined hundreds of girls. Believe me, if you go to his aunt's house, you'd see what I mean. If you force me to go with him, how will you answer to God? Or the Committee?"

As I went over to talk to Mother privately, Zeynab's eyes followed me intently and she stared at us as we conferred. Her face was in a constant state of flux, like undulating forms on the surface of water, making it hard to fathom what lay beneath them. Her expression reflected fear and hope, sincerity and mischief. She looked so pitiful, and I felt simultaneously drawn to her and repulsed by her. Something enigmatic and mysterious pulsated from her that bewitched and frightened me at the same time—like dark unchartered terrain, full of promise and temptation but impenetrable and menacing, a disturbing dream unbound by the norms of reason and convention.

Once again, Zeynab looked guileless and vulnerable, moving in my direction to seek aid and solace. With eyes brimming with tears, in a voice soft and plaintive she whispered, "In the shower I was talking to God. I am not kidding. I don't say my prayers because I don't know the words but I talk to God. When Mohammad Agha brought me here, I thought I was going to heaven. Your mother was an angel. So were you. I was crying in the shower, telling God, they are good people; I must tell them the truth. Mohammad Agha told me not to open my mouth, or I'd be kicked out. But something made me talk. I couldn't lie to you folks."

I was moved to uncertainty. She was telling the truth. Even if she wasn't, I had an overwhelming urge to believe her. I wanted her and her words to lower my defenses and overcome my resistance.

"This girl is crazy and a pathological liar. She has no idea who she is and where she comes from," Mother had determined.

Perhaps, I thought. But who were we, I asked myself, with all the genealogical charts and documented vital dates, well-defined thoughts, carefully assessed plans, clearly demarcated philosophical grounds, trivial pursuits, and major apprehensions, who were we?

"Zeynab will stay with us," I rumbled across the room. "We will not turn her over to anyone." Mother was so shocked by my announcement she could have been knocked down by a feather. But before she could raise her voice, I repeated the verdict. My heart palpitated with an undefinable exhilaration.

Wordlessly, Mohammad Agha finished the tea and stood up. He mumbled something by way of leave-taking and departed. As soon as the door closed behind him, Zeynab gave a shrill yelp and began laughing, laughing spasmodically and endlessly. I could not tell if she was laughing with joy or having made a dupe out of me. It did not matter. I had done my deed and was happy about it. I had an urge to make her sit down and tell me her stories. I could also tell her the stories I had buried deep inside me. Perhaps Mother's plan of marrying her off to a decent man who could be put to work for my brother and sending their offspring abroad for education, etc., could now be implemented.

We sat down to lunch in an eerie silence. We were all deep in thought, as if trying to make sense of the events of the past few days. None of us felt at ease.

Around four in the afternoon, Zeynab awoke from

a nap and sat upright. "I had a terrible dream," she announced cheerlessly, but did not elaborate.

Around sunset, a telephone call came from the young man, the employee of Ghods Department Store. He wanted to talk to Zeynab. Mother, like someone suddenly awakened from a sleep, was dazed and confused. She stared at me quizzically. From outside there were sounds of shouting and sporadic gunfire. I felt the onset of an anxiety attack and tried to collect my thoughts. Mother hurriedly drew the curtains tight and locked the front door, her face contorted with worry. Zeynab took the receiver and listened without saying a word. She seemed wan, and a bitter, defiant look came over her face. Her eyes lost that childlike impetuosity, looking more like those of a mature woman crushed under the weight of experience. She handed the receiver to my mother and said blankly, "I am leaving."

As she went to fetch her bag, the man explained to my mother that his brother had decided to marry Zeynab. Their mother, a pious woman, he remarked, would like to keep her for a while. He added that, God willing, we would be invited to the wedding.

"Wonderful, congratulations," intoned Mother reflexively. "Every young girl must marry someday."

"Easy for you to say," said Zeynab, almost disgustedly.

"Listen," I told her urgently. "You don't have to go if you don't want to. Wait, my brother knows the Committee chief."

"What Committee?" she said sneeringly.

"So," I spat out, hurt and angry, "all that talk of a marriage and the department store employee is another one of your fabrications, huh?"

"What difference does it make?" she replied coldly, as she moved toward the door. "Unlucky folks are unlucky wherever they go."

At the front door, she turned and gazed in my direction. "In my dream this afternoon," she said, "I was in heaven, when a hand reached out and grabbed my hair and said I didn't belong there. I belonged in hell. I knew right there and then that I had to go."

I wanted so badly to stop her. I wanted for once to do something from the heart, something fantastic and irrational, but was immobilized with indecision, not able to find the courage to act.

"What do you think," asked Mother. "Was she telling the truth?"

GOLI TARAGHI is a well-known and widely read novelist in Iran. Her works have been translated into several languages. Her latest collection of short stories, *The Pomegranate Lady and her Sons*, was recently published in the United States. Born in Tehran, Taraghi was educated in Iran and the United States, and presently lives in France.

Mermaid Café

Mitra Eliyati

ONE BY ONE all the taverns and cafés in our small seaside town were shut down. The only one left was the Mermaid Café. Now a crowd of angry townsfolk was gathering in front of it. I was there with my buddy, Sohrab, waiting to see if the mob would attack the café. We thought we would rush in, and rescue the mermaid by lifting her off her perch above the doorway and running out the back door.

From where we were, we could hear her melancholy song. She was singing with such sadness it almost made me cry. The light from the naked bulb hanging over the door glistened off the slicked-back hair of the guys leaving the café.

Uncle Yusef had promised to take me to the Mermaid Café if I got high grades and finished top of my class. This never happened, because my father disapproved of the idea. "Not a place for kids and such," he had ruled.

"This damn place should be closed down," I heard Haj Yadollah's voice behind me. He then told the women to stay away. There were some children milling around among the adults.

Two men, in black hats, went into the café. They slammed the door behind them so hard that the mermaid with the goblet in her hand was visibly shaken.

Every time I passed the café, I pretended I did not look at the mermaid's golden locks and curvaceous body.

Now I surveyed the crowd and saw that our head-master and some upper-classmates from our school had joined in, ready for action.

Sohrab tapped me on the shoulder. "Look over there," he said, "There's your dad."

Sure enough, there he was by the newsstand talking with some men from work. He looked upset.

"Darn it!" I blurted out. "I think we're in trouble."

"What do we do now?"

"Duck your head. Maybe he won't see us."

"What then? He ain't blind."

It occurred to me he might be there to protect the café. After all, he was a regular customer.

"More trouble," Sohrab warned.

"What's the matter now?"

"Hussein Jumbo and his gang!"

"You're kidding."

"I swear on my father's grave," he said. "You've got eyes. Look for yourself."

Sure enough, they were approaching from a side street, waving clubs and sticks over their heads.

"They're welcome," I bragged, pretending not to be intimidated.

"Let's get the hell outta here."

"Over my dead body," I said, defiantly.

"Gutsy again, huh?" Sohrab sneered. "Have you forgotten about that night?"

THE NIGHT SOHRAB was referring to had happened the previous summer when we were hanging out and had noticed the new bouncer in front of Mermaid Café. He was such a big fellow that he could block the whole doorway with his body. He refused admittance to Hussein Jumbo and his gang.

"Monsieur's[1] orders," he boomed.

"You must be kidding," said one of the boys.

"You're asking for it," said another, menacingly.

The bouncer remained unmoved. He stepped aside reverently, allowing two regular customers in.

The gang members, standing to the side of the café in relative darkness, kept taunting the bouncer, hurling insults at him. One of them, known as Abbas the Loner, stepped out of the dark, staggering. "I'm going in," he announced boldly. "Get lost, out of my way," he said, but he stepped back when he saw the size of the bouncer.

[1] An informal way of referring to male Armenians and members of other Christian sects in Iran. Here, it is referring to the café owner.

Another member, short and plump, rushed toward the café entrance. From his pants pocket he produced a switchblade knife and pointed it threateningly at the gigantic bouncer—from a safe distance. "To hell with Monsieur. I'm coming in," he yelled at the bouncer, who beckoned to him to come forward.

Sohrab, standing next to me behind the boxwood hedge, was excited, anticipating the spectacle of a free-for-all between the bouncer and the gang. He started laughing uncontrollably. He was almost bent double in a paroxysm of laughter, attracting the attention of Hussein Jumbo, who ordered his gang to come after us. We sensed the danger and ran as fast as we could down the back alleys and if it hadn't been for Mozaffari the policeman nearby, we would have been torn to pieces.

SOHRAB TAPPED ME on the shoulder. "They'll recognize us, don't you think?" he asked anxiously, pointing to Hussein Jumbo and his gang.

"Suppose they do. What of it?" I answered, trying to sound unconcerned.

"Remember? You soiled your pants that night," he said.

"Shut your trap! Or I'll chop your head off."

"All right, I'll shut up. But it looks like we're in deep shit."

I looked back and noticed Hussein and his gang working their way through the crowd to get a closer position.

"I have an idea," said Sohrab.

"Then come out with it."

"What's the point? You don't take me seriously."

"Come on, spit it out," I hissed, impatiently.

Sohrab scratched his head and cleared his throat. "What if we join the headmaster?" he mused.

That was a stupid idea: Sohrab knew that the headmaster had lodged complaints against the café, demanding its removal from the vicinity of the school.

"You always say such dumb things!" I fulminated. "The headmaster is already a part of the mob, you jackass."

We heard a loud, scratchy voice proclaim, "Tear the place down!"

"God is great!" Haj Yadollah excitedly cried.

"So, now you call me a jackass," Sohrab said plaintively.

I almost punched his face because I felt he was trying to extricate himself from the situation. Then I would be left alone to rescue the mermaid from the vicious mob.

"You can't take a joke, can you?" I said amicably, holding tight to his wrist.

Then I heard the unmistakable voice of Hussein Jumbo. "We must set fire to this corrupt, rotten joint," he shouted loudly.

"All it takes is a can of gasoline and a box of matches," suggested one of the boys in the gang.

"Then what are we waiting for?" someone with a scratchy voice yelled.

Suddenly, Sohrab jerked his hand out of my grip.

"What the hell do you want from me?" he asked contentiously. "What does all this have to do with me? What's in it for me, anyway?"

"You can get her lute," I told him, trying to be conciliatory.

"What good is it to me? I can't play."

"You can sell it. It's a collector's item, worth a lot of money."

Several men walked out of the café, frightened at the sight of the crowd, and frenetically hurried down a dark alley. Two members of Hussein's gang ran after them and disappeared in the darkness.

"I'll give you two tomans over and above," I offered Sohrab.

"That's a deal," he replied.

The gangs who had followed the customers in the alley returned carrying a container between them. The crowd parted to let them in.

"Don't you dare start a fire," warned Haj Yadollah, waving his walking stick over his head vigorously. "Somebody stop these bastards." He tried to push his way toward them in the middle of the crowd. Some people followed him.

"Let's go help Haj Yadollah," I urged Sohrab.

"But didn't you say he was one of them?" he asked, exasperated.

I was confused, unable to think straight. Sohrab was

trying to pull me behind him by my sleeve. "Let's move on. Let's get going," he insisted.

As we pondered the idea, I noticed a hand slowly push aside the curtain on the window of the café. I watched, motionless.

"It's her," I whispered, my heart thumping.

"Who?" asked Sohrab.

"The mermaid!"

"Who?"

She was just as I had imagined her.

"Can't you hear?" Sohrab uttered irritably. "Who? I asked."

The time had stopped still. I could not make a sound.

"She is the same woman who is there every night," Sohrab speculated. He did not know what he was talking about. The woman behind the window was the mermaid herself, the one I had seen in my dreams. She wiggled like a fish and dove into the sea as I tried to embrace her.

By now the crowd was behind us, pushing us forward. Some men started whistling.

"Stop it," Haj Yadollah yelled, sounding outraged.

"We must stone her," the man with the scratchy voice announced.

"God is great!" Haj Yadollah responded.

The woman in the window crossed herself and let the curtain drop.

Somebody hurled a rock at the mermaid over the door

of the café. It hit the goblet in her hand and shattered it. The bouncer poked his head out of the door and surveyed the crowd.

"Who the hell is throwing rocks?" he yelled piercingly. Not receiving a satisfactory answer, he swung the door open and walked out with a broken bottle in his hand.

"Whoever is throwing rocks," he shouted angrily. "I'll rip his guts out."

Women screamed as they retreated behind the relative safety of boxwood hedges. Children scattered all over the square.

A contingent of policemen headed by Mozaffari arrived on the scene as the owner gathered the shards of the broken goblet. The crowd began to disperse.

For three days Mozaffari didn't move from his post in front of the café. He looked glum. He did not smile as he usually did, displaying his two gold front teeth.

After that night I was stricken with high fever that kept me in bed for a month. Everybody suspected typhoid and feared for my life.

Soon, trees blossomed and streets were cleaned. But there was no longer a trace of the Mermaid Café, or Mozaffari and his men.

Monsieur had left the neighborhood and the mermaid holding a broken goblet had disappeared.

MITRA ELIYATI is an award-winning writer and poet, and the recipient of Golshiri Literary Prize. Eliyati is the author of two short story collections, *Mademoiselle Katie* and *The Mermaid Café*. She is the founder and editor of a literary website, *Jennie and Fairy*, and writes for several literary journals. She teaches and lives in Tehran.

Unsettled, Unbound

Fariba Vafi

THE MOVING TRUCK is late. I have arranged a row of cardboard boxes against the wall on one side of the room. Mammad's mother is feeding the baby in a corner near the window. The baby lifts her hand to grab the spoon and feed herself. The old woman looks uncomfortable, perspiring heavily under her chador. Mr. Yazdani keeps talking incessantly, foam forming at the corners of his mouth. Mother keeps saying, "Yes, yes, of course," as if she is listening to the old man's chatter, but she is hoping he would stop talking and leave the room, so she could remove her chador to cool off. Finally Mr. Yazdani steps out and she rips the chador off her head, relieved. She then turns to me, her face registering concern.

"Why are you leaving?" she asks, disapproval in her tone. "Your children will be unsettled," she tells me. I feel like laughing when she says "children," considering one is still in my belly. She's been saying that ever since she learned I was leaving Mr. Yazdani's house. Hearing the word "unsettled" from her mouth gives me a sense of release. The word does not evoke any negative implications in me as she certainly intends it to do. It makes me think instead of a wandering, free-spirited dervish, not a homeless vagrant. As for the "children," I have no idea how to react. I feel I am in transition. Leila lives in Tehran and has helped us find a house to rent.

I haven't been sleeping well. I am worried and anxious. Things can go either way. Mammad may call and say that it is not a good idea for me to move to Tehran, that he made a mistake in agreeing with my plans, that it is not easy to live in Tehran, that it is a mistake to leave our own town and province. Or, like he did the last time, nix my idea altogether and say, "Why do you want to move?" To which I would have to reply, "You are already away from your own town and province," and talk about my loneliness, pointing out the fact that Tehran is closer to where he works and he can come home more often, every two weeks or so.

Everyday I pack the boxes I have picked up from the corner grocer. I label them with their contents and place them against the wall. I still have a lot of packing to do. By now I am exhausted and careless about what goes into each carton. I just fill them up and line them against the wall.

Mr. Yazdani is a constant, bothersome presence. He is one of those old men who feel entitled to interfere in everybody's life. His gray hair has now yellowed with age. He has a florid complexion that looks flushed when he talks. He has strangely hirsute hands. He always looks harassed and there is an urgency in his movements. One would think that at the time of his death he would hurry things up to get a more desirable place in the ever after.

The first time I saw Mr. Yazdani, his watchful eyes darting under puffy eyelids, I had a premonition. He always seemed like he was chasing you with his eyes, constantly watching every move. But the house was attractive and I couldn't resist because of its bothersome landlord. It took me a while to convince Mammad. He was likely to change his mind at any time, and insist that in his absence the best place for me and the baby would be his mother's house.

Mr. Yazdani had his acquisitive gaze fixed on me, trying to look understanding and sympathetic as Mammad signed the lease. We were now Yazdani's tenants and Mammad stayed for a few days before going back to work. The first day, Mrs. Yazdani, with her half-covered face under the chador, turned to Mammad and exchanged greetings and pleasantries with him. She then turned the uncovered half of her face to me.

"I told Yazdani that only one child is allowed," she said, as she glanced at my swelling belly. Mammad had told her that we would soon be a family of four. "Well now that you are here," she added, "it doesn't matter. You are all welcome."

The Yazdanis had two sons living at home and attending college. They seemed very shy. Any time we met on the staircase, they would stand aside against the wall and slide down the stairs, eyes cast downward.

Since our apartment was on the first floor, we could hear the traffic up and down the staircase. Visitors were supposed to take their shoes off before ascending the carpeted stairs to the Yazdani residence. We could often hear Mr. Yazdani grumble audibly for the untidy way shoes had been left at the bottom of the staircase. He picked them up and neatly arranged them by the wall.

I fell in love with the place at first sight. It was quiet and afforded privacy. The rooms were freshly painted, sunny, and inviting. The kitchen was large with a window opening onto the alley. When I opened the window I could hear the birds singing. The alley was wide and clean, with old houses on either side. The house across from our kitchen window was well-kept, and its wall was covered with jasmine and musk-scented roses. In the afternoons, a little girl would come out to play in her toy car. With the baby in my arms, I would watch her from the window, as she appreciated the audience, pedaling faster and doing intricate maneuvers around the courtyard.

Mr. Yazdani handed me the basement key. "Dear girl, consider this your own home," he said.

"Thank you," I replied.

"You're like my own daughter."

"Thank you."

I had said "Thank you" one hundred times to get rid of him, but Yazdani had to explain the house rules over and over again. There were certain conditions for the use of the yard. The shoe rack had to be placed at a certain angle at the entrance door. I could use the garden hose, but had to roll it up and hang it on the hook every time. He talked hurriedly and in a low whisper, putting his face close to my face, staring at me with inquisitive eyes, as if he was searching for some unknown secret. I could see the pupils of his eyes moving restlessly from side to side.

I had become aware of the old man's disturbing energy early on. He was unlike other elderly men who would slump down in a comfortable chair and doze off. Actually, I don't remember ever seeing him seated at all. He was always in motion, climbing up or down the stairs, or on his way somewhere. Every time I ran into him, he made a point of letting me know he was late to some important appointment, apologizing for not being able to stop for a chat, but half an hour later, he would appear again to greet me as if he had not seen me in ages and he had been longing for this encounter. Several times every morning and evening, he would knock on my door and apologize profusely for having been remiss in checking on me and offering his services.

Manizheh and Maliheh, the young sisters of Mammad, always hung around the hallway to run into Mr. Yazdani. They were so amused by his eccentricity. It was like they were watching a movie. They engaged him in conversation and later mimicked his mannerisms.

"Your landlord is a real gentleman," they told me.

The "real gentleman" always held himself upright more elegantly than usual to bid farewell to them at the door. Sometimes he invited the young guests to stay for dinner or lunch upstairs. The exchange of compliments usually continued for some time before the young girls took their leave. The girls believed that the wife must be ugly and unpleasant. For some reason, I always took the side of the wife and expounded on her intelligence and exquisite taste. She was not beautiful in the conventional sense, I told the girls, but she was uniquely attractive. I always thought, what if Mrs. Yazdani happened to come down the stairs and run into Manizheh and Maliheh, who seemed to take my description of Mrs. Yazdani with a grain of salt, wondering why Mr. Yazdani, this darling of a man, spent so much time downstairs if he had an angel for a wife upstairs.

Mrs. Yazdani was always warm and receptive to Mammad's mother. "Dear lady," she told her. "Visit your daughter-in-law more often."

Before long, Mr. Yazdani knew one by one of the family members and friends that visited me at the apartment. He even had figured out the texture of my relationship with each. My mother-in-law approved of this level of close attention paid by Mr. Yazdani to my affairs. I could often hear her expressions of gratitude from the alley in the extended process of leave-taking. I would hug the baby and watch from the window as the guests departed. I felt an innate desire to leave with them. But I would be brought back to the reality of my situation when I heard Yazdani as he cleaned the hallway and organized the shoes along the wall. To me, he had become an intrusive burden. The apartment that was once so welcoming, had become like a prison and, Mr. Yazdani like a vigilant prison warden, who guarded it incessantly.

Close to the sunset every evening there is a knock on my door.

"Yes?" I almost bark, knowing who is likely on the other side.

"It's me, my daughter."

I crack the door. He thrusts in his hand, holding a loaf of flat bread.

"But thanks," I say. "We have enough bread in the house."

"Take it anyway, dear girl. I bought it especially for you. It is fresh. This is something your husband would have done, had he been here. But he is not. You see?"

There is no point in refusing the offer. So I take the bread. "Thank you and goodnight," I mutter, trying to close the door. But he pleads for just a minute of my time to share "some very important information." That means I have to listen to his gibberish for another half hour and be told again how happy he is to have a virtuous young lady like me as his tenant. So different from his former tenants, a couple that did not get along and quarreled all the time, ruining the reputation of the house in the neighborhood. He would then spend more time apologizing for assailing my sensibilities by the use of such words as "slut," "shameless," and "shrew" in reference to his previous tenant. I am such an angel in nature and disposition that I should consider myself as the owner of the property and him as a mere caretaker. Somehow, I am defenseless against his intrusions. I promise myself to never accept anything from such an importunate, irritating man.

In their late teens, with clear complexions and hazel eyes, Manizheh and Maliheh were attractive. It gave them immense pleasure to have the old man stand reverentially in front of them and admire their youthful charm using quaint, archaic terms. His age and theatrical demeanor were amusing to them and his polite manner had put him beyond any suspicion, but the girls were curious to meet his wife, something that wasn't forthcoming, given Mrs. Yazdani's reluctance to mingle and her self-imposed isolation upstairs.

Once the girls came up with the idea of going to a fortuneteller. There was an Armenian lady who lived in the neighborhood and was well known for telling fortunes by reading coffee grinds. Everyone called her "Madame."

I wanted no part of it. "I don't want to have my fortune told," I said. "It is not fair for all of us to show up and only one pay for her services." The girls were amused by my hesitancy. "Don't worry," said one of them, snickering. "We will keep your secrets."

"We could all three have our fortunes told," was the decision.

Madame's front yard was immaculately kept with flowers and greeneries. The consulting room upstairs was dimly lit. It took us a few minutes to get used to the low light. We sat around a table and looked at an elegant cupboard full of antique china and ceramic dishes and receptacles. Madame watched us from the top of her spectacles and asked how many cups of coffee we wanted. She then left the room and returned with three cups on a tray. The aroma of coffee set off in me a bout of craving.

It was Maliheh's turn first. She kept glancing at us, clicking her tongue as Madame talked, indicating her astonishment at the veracity of Madame's prognostications. Manizheh, on the other hand, was not quite so impressed.

"And then what will happen, Madame?" she asked, when Madame stopped talking. There was a touch of skepticism in her voice.

"You will come into some money on two occasions," Madame declared gravely.

"A whole bunch of money, or what?"

"I can't tell. But it will be on two occasions. They may be apart two days, two weeks, two months . . ." Madame answered, allowing her voice to trail.

My turn was last. Madame picked my cup and held it up close to my face. The girls craned their necks to see. The grounds had formed into a crisscrossing of tracks and roads.

"Your heart is not here," she said. "You are a stranger

in your own house. You will be leaving this place in a near future."

"Where is she going, Madame?" the girls asked in unison, clearly enjoying to let the word "Madame" roll off their tongues.

"I don't know. But she is going," Madame answered.

"Perhaps you have some secret plans we know nothing about," said Maliheh, looking at me askance.

"I have a secret plan to make a beautiful quilt," I said, grinning and pointing to my belly.

THE GIRLS ENJOYED talking about household goods and furnishings. Every time they came for a visit they commented on the pillows in the guest room. In this visit they had concluded that I needed new pillowcases because they showed their age.

"Polyester fill is better for pillows," Maliheh opined.

"Wool is the best," Manizheh interjected.

"Then I need to know what to do with all the feathers I have got in mine," I said jokingly. This made us all laugh.

"We should have gone to the store today to buy pillowcases for feather pillows," one of them suggested.

MANIZHEH WAS STILL upset about her conversation with Madame. "That was a waste of money," she complained.

I found myself in agreement with her. "She put me in the mood for travel," I said.

"Perhaps you miss your dear husband," said Manizheh, winking suggestively, "so you want to go see him, huh?"

Almost always there was something racy in their comments and body language when they spoke about husbands, matrimony, and such matters.

"He's going to be here in a few days," I said. "No need for me to go see him."

Then we started mimicking Madame. We all thought she was rather miserly in dispensing coffee in those tiny mugs. The girls were pleased and said theirs were good but yours—instead of babies and birds in your cup—was roads and highways. We all laughed.

After I saw my guests off at the top of the alley, I returned home, picked up the baby, and headed for the park to have a stroll and some ice cream. Afterward, near the playground, I plumped down on a bench next to an old women who sat motionless, staring into the empty space. The child left my side and went to play on the slide. For some reason I thought of the winding roads and tracks on the bottom of the coffee cup and Madame's predictions. Was it possible that I might leave this place for somewhere else? The only thing I had not thought about in recent years was leaving, going somewhere. It occurred to me that I had always trained myself to stay put, to remain static. In my mind I had sealed off all the possible exits to alternative modes of existence.

The sun had already set when I got home, but Mr. Yazdani was still there at the entrance to the house. When he saw me he struck a pose as if he was about to recite an ode. I felt depressed. I said hello and rushed into the apartment, locking the door behind me. A few minutes later he was knocking on the door, offering his company as an antidote to my loneliness.

The old man had discovered in me a solitude and innocence that he desired to be part of and share. At every encounter he would smile at me and ruefully shake his head. Throughout the day he would frequently stop by the apartment and ask if there was anything he could do for me. He would consider it a privilege to be of service. I always had to cut him off. "I beg your pardon," I would say and shut the door. On leaving the house, I had to make sure he was not anywhere near the hallway. I would bundle the baby, letting her know that we had to be quiet. We would move noiselessly to the door and reach for the lock, key in hand. Even so, more often than not he would materialize behind me and offer to help me open the door. "There is a trick to it," he would say. "You can't handle it by yourself."

Occasionally, Mrs. Yazdani would descend to the world below her upstairs domain. She was openly contemptuous of her husband and the way he looked. "In his seventies and he still wore tight jeans with a big belt buckle," she would grumble. "He always smelled of a very strong cologne. He combed what was left of his gray hair on the sides of his head to cover the bald patch on his skull." She found all that disgusting.

"He's become very effeminate," she told me once. "He spends more time in front of the mirror than a woman."

For her part, Mrs. Yazdani had given up on her femininity. She didn't pluck her eyebrows. She simply gathered her untended hair over her head in a shapeless bun. A black hair grew out of a mole on her cheek, tempting one to reach out and pluck it. She had missing teeth. A lifetime of discontent had tracked her face with lines of a permanent frown that did not dissipate even when she smiled on rare occasions.

When Mammad came for a visit on a weekend, I told him about my problem with Mr. Yazdani.

"Do you mean he is a lecher?" he wanted to know.

"No, he's not," I replied emphatically, although deep down, I wasn't quite sure.

"You should be able to regulate your relationship with others," he said. "I can do it for you, if you can't."

"I can," I said, and then changed the subject.

Mammad left the next day. I limited my outing, as I knew Mr. Yazdani was always hovering in the background like a phantom watching my every move. I imagined myself as an assertive woman who would resolutely walk up to him, handing back the house key, silence him with a stern glare, and walk away. He would be shaken by surprise, and speechless like a mute.

Once I ran into Madame on my way back to the house.

"You are still here?" she asked, genuinely surprised.

"I've just arrived," was the only rejoinder I could think of. "Why should I want to leave?"

It occurred to me that I really did not have any other place to go.

In bed at night, I often touched my belly to feel the movement of the baby inside. Sometimes I did not immediately detect any motion. I would be overcome with fear that the fetus was dead. I held my breath until I felt some movement, softly kicking the walls of my womb, some indication of a growing, thriving life.

But that night it was not an anxiety attack I was experiencing. It was an overwhelming excitement, as if my whole body was charged with a renewed energy, a sense of liveliness filling my entire body. It was not an unknown feeling, but it took me a while to recognize the same sensation I had once experienced before.

The sea was tranquil and shimmering in the sunlight. I was lounging under a parasol painted with a sunflower design. The beach was crowded with people, some stretched on the sand, others afloat in the sea, their heads bobbing up and down in the gentle waves. I moved closer to the sea. I did not know how to swim. I sat on the warm, wet sand and stretched my legs as water caressed my naked feet. The wet sand felt warm and soft under my feet. I stretched out on my back, looking at the blue sky. Nobody seemed to notice me, as if I was a part of the scenery. I felt integrated with all around me, feeling the living presence of the sea, the thrill of being alone and forgotten, floating between earth and sky, savoring the deep peace within. I am alone, and I am free, drifting here and there, following the whims of the wind, going wherever it chooses. I had never felt that sense of freedom, that transcendence, before. I had a sensation of being suspended in the wind, gliding over the waves like seagulls effortlessly on currents of air. I was overcome with a sense of gratitude. I was grateful to the sea, to the earth, to the sky, savoring that deep peace offered me, trilled with joy as being a part of the natural world. I had a vague, indescribable awareness of being completely free. It superseded any notions of freedom I had had before.

My heart was racing and the novelty of the experience, the overwhelming beauty of existence, brought tears to my eyes. There was something sacred about it. I promised myself never to forget the exhilaration of that moment, to let it be the guiding light of my life, to live free and never allow the darkness and sorrows of the world to drive that sense of freedom out of me.

I was not able to keep that promise. I convinced myself that the experience was due to too much sun and the sea air. But that night, in the bleak, enclosed space of the room, I felt it again. The gentle movements of the fetus in my womb imbued me with the power of being in harmony with an infinite universe. I got up and pulled the blanket over the baby sleeping in her crib. I opened the window slowly and took a deep breath of the night air, redolent with the fragrance of the jasmine. I did not know what time it was. The lights were out and the night was quiet. Only the muffled chorus of crickets broke the silence of the night.

I saw a tiny speck of light at the far end of the yard. It was the glowing tip of a cigarette. Immediately I recognized the silhouette of a man squatting by the flower-bed holding it. It was Mr. Yazdani. I jumped back reflexively, fearing detection. But the old man was in his own world, oblivious to his surroundings. It was strange to see him silent and motionless. I closed the window and went back to bed.

A day or so later, there was a knock on the door. It was Yazdani. By now I recognized his knock. It had a certain rhythmic quality about it. It brought to my mind a picture of him standing in the hall preparing a flood of words to unleash on me when I opened the door. His confidence that I would open the door engulfed me and made me reach for the doorknob. But something stopped my hand in midair.

I did not open the door.

After a few more knocks on the door, with varying degrees of force, Yazdani gave up and left. An hour later the telephone rang. I reached for the plug and pulled it out of the socket, somehow knowing that it was Mr. Yazdani. He had called several times before. I returned to the kitchen and slumped in a chair. I did not feel like doing anything.

I don't know how long it was before I heard a knock

on the door. I was startled by it, although I had been hearing movement in the hall. I went over to the baby's room and closed the door so she wouldn't be awakened by the noise.

I stood next to the door, my heart racing. Inside me, I could feel the movement of the fetus, strengthening my determination not to open the door.

Now Mrs. Yazdani was downstairs knocking on the door. She slapped the door with the palm of her hand, calling me by name. The couple had probably seen me come in, and knew that I had not left the apartment. In the background I heard the voice of one of their sons. They were having a heated exchange among them but I could not figure out what they were saying. After a few minutes they gave up and went upstairs.

I heaved a deep sigh of relief.

It was early evening when I was transfixed by the sound of a key turning in the front-door lock. Then I saw the handle move. I rushed toward the baby's room, standing in front of it defensively. The door opened slowly and Mr. Yazdani's head with its shock of gray hair poked into the room. He glanced around and was surprised to see me. I screamed loudly, involuntarily.

By now he was inside the room with hands raised in an attempt to calm me down. A stream of words were pouring out of his mouth so fast I wasn't able to comprehend. Finally, he paused briefly. "Forgive me, please," he said, articulating every word. "I didn't mean any harm."

Now Mrs. Yazdani came down the stairs, shouting "What's the matter? What's the matter?"

She had her husband's striped pajama bottoms on but no chador. "What the hell?" she yelled at her husband, and rushed to embrace me.

"He made a mistake," she said. "He meant no harm."

The baby had been awakened by the commotion. She drifted into the living room, rubbing her eyes. Mrs. Yazdani swept her off her feet and thrust her into my arms. "Please, calm down. You're scaring the baby," she said.

Mr. Yazdani was more intensely red in the face than ever before, his eyes sunken in their sockets. He was foaming at the mouth. "I thought something had happened to the innocent child," he managed to say.

Mrs. Yazdani pushed him out of the room and headed for the kitchen. She came back with a glass full of sugar water and forced me to drink it. She then took my hand and pressed it to her breast. The baby had stopped crying, but kept her arms tightly around my neck. Mrs. Yazdani told me not to move as she left the room, only to return a few minutes later carrying a plate full of fresh plump apricots. She picked one, split it in halves, giving me one and the baby the other half. The intense orange hue inside the fruit indicated that it was ripe. It was from her own tree in the garden, she informed me.

"Mr. Yazdani has gotten old and senile," she said in a sorrowful tone. "He is scared of death and does weird things. He is miserable. He is in the yard hitting himself on the head, crying. You can go see for yourself if you don't believe me. Forgive him out of the goodness of your heart."

She asked me not mention the incident to my husband. When I assured her I wouldn't, she got up and left.

The next day I ran into Mr. Yazdani in the hallway. It was not a chance encounter by any means; it was obvious he had been waiting for me. He looked older and more decrepit than before. With a deep bow and in a tone more stilted than ever he addressed me: "My dear daughter, I was apprehensive of the welfare of your precious little darling. I had no intention of intruding," he began, and then proceeded to give an account of the accidental death of a relative by gas poisoning, an incident which he said was his motive to check on me. He followed the narrative by repeated pleas to forgive him, despite my own repeated assurances that I had. He held me up in the hall until his wife called him upstairs.

I think it was at that moment that I decided to move.

I am jolted by Mammad's mother calling me. We are standing in the middle of a roomful of boxes. "How can you move all this singlehandedly?" she wonders, looking around. She continues, "Some folks are not very helpful. They always come for dinners and receptions but not when they are expected to help." I don't know who is the target of her invective.

"Not a big deal," I say, trying to make light of the

situation. "We'll throw everything in the truck and let it go at that."

Mr. Yazdani comes into the room, excitedly reporting the arrival of the truck, a fact of which we are already aware. To initiate the loading process, my mother-in-law tries to pick up one of the boxes. I pull her back. "It is too heavy," I warn. "Don't even think about it."

"Not you, either," she says, pointing to my protruding belly.

We are milling among the boxes, trying to come up with a way of packing them into the truck.

"Hello," I hear a voice behind me. I turn around. It is a friend of mine and her husband. For a moment I think they are apparitions. I had never asked anybody for help with moving. But they had come on their own initiative and—what is more—they had brought a few more friends with them. Mammad's mother, looking relieved, picks up the baby and moves out of the way.

Mr. Yazdani, in his usual harried and hasty manner comes into the room. "Are you sure you haven't packed the garden hose?" he wants to know. I simply point to it on the hook in the yard.

My friends roll up the carpet in the living room and hoist it up to the bed of the truck where a few of them are standing, working out a strategy to make the best use of available space. From the window I look at them. They are young men, their light-hearted banter echoing in the narrow alley.

I haven't done such a good job of packing, although I have moved several times in my life. A plastic bag over-stuffed with bathroom items bursts and disgorges its contents, among them an unsightly oversized ewer, made of red plastic. For some reason, the young men find the object amusing. They all laugh heartily. I try to share in their merriment, but I can't. Somehow, I am embarrassed by the plastic baby bathtub, plastic ball, plastic soap dish strewn on the bed of the truck, as if I am defined by them. Why didn't I throw them away, leave them behind? By the same token, why don't I dispose of all those sentiments, emotions, precepts that crowd my mind? Can I ever be rid of them?

A young man is holding up the red ewer over his head for further amusement and fun. I feel a sharp pain in my back and the onset of despair. Would that ewer be sus-pended up there forever as an emblem of my existence? Finally, the ewer loses its entertainment value and is packed away out of sight, but I do not feel any relief from the painful bite of its symbolism.

In the meantime, Mr. Yazdani keeps going in and out of the apartment trying to be a part of the packing activ-ities, but being more of a distraction and a nuisance. "I want to make sure you don't leave anything behind," he tells me.

Now fully packed, the truck moves slowly out of the alley, onto the main thoroughfare. I have already said goodbye to Mrs. Yazdani. All I have to do is turn over the key to Mr. Yazdani and get back my security deposit. I have been waiting for this moment.

He is standing by the door holding his hand to his forehead to shade his eyes against the afternoon sun. He looks flushed in the heat of the day. I move toward him with my head down looking at his belt buckle—and the belt, which is frayed by age. I hand him the key and pull the check from his fingers. I avoid eye contact, not wanting to see the expression on his face. Not that it matters anymore. "All the best, dear girl," he mumbles.

Slowly, I walk away. I wish he were not standing there so I could look back at the house and the alley once more. I already miss Madame, the little girl from across the alley, the climbing musk roses and jasmines. I resist the urge to look back. The sun is hot and the truck has now maneuvered itself out of the alley, easing its way into the traffic. I catch a glimpse of the household goods under the tarpaulin. I pick up the baby in my arms and walk toward the taxicab. I will be at the bus terminal within the hour.

FARIBA VAFI is a best-selling author of several novels and short story collections. Her novel, *My Bird*, was winner of the Yalda and Golshiri Literary Awards in Iran for best novel of the year in 2002, and was translated and published in English, German, and Italian. Vafi lives in Tehran.

The Burnt Sound

Behnaz Alipour Gaskari

AFTER THE FIRE in the solitary cell block, we were moved to another location in the prison. The fire, which had started in the auto repair shop adjacent to the prison wall, rapidly spread to the cell block. Through the skylight we could see the flames raging. After many years, I can still hear women's cries for help, and screams of fear muffled by the roaring fire and billowing smoke.

After sunset, when the usual noise of the cell block would die down somewhat, a flock of rooks would set off crowing. As if on cue, the boy would start singing, loud enough to come across the prison wall. His undulating voice sounded familiar and appealing. I was a girl in solitary confinement, and he was most likely, an awkward shy boy, working in the auto body shop next to the prison. He had an Azary[1] accent and his musical voice kept beat with the rhythm of his steps crunching on the sandy floor of the workshop. I cherished the sound. I would pace my cell

---

[1] The accent of the natives of Azarbaijan, the northwestern province of Iran.

in rapid steps, circling around in ecstasy to the point of feeling dizzy and nauseous. The sound had come to mean the world to me. Like a frog lunging at every gnat buzzing in the air, I would listen intently for every decibel of sound coming through the wall.

> —What are you dragging your feet for? The tea is brewed. Don't you see?
> —What?
> —What do you mean what? Pour two cups for me and the gentleman.

I could hear his hurrying footsteps on the floor. I could imagine him sitting on a bench or leaning against the wall waiting for orders. I could hear him coughing, and snatches of his conversation with others in the shop. Sometimes a smell not unlike a whiff of burned grass would drift into the cell, suggesting some cheap tea being brewed on the other side of the wall. Then there were unsteady footfalls as of a drunk shuffling, followed by the boy chuckling, then his peals of laughter. The sounds reached my ears as if echoed from the surrounding hills. I would smile involuntarily despite the listlessness and clenched teeth set off by the cold prison cell and the morning chill that suppressed any appetite for breakfast. I just listened for the crunching sound of the boy's footfall as I squatted in a corner of the cell hugging my knees and staring at the graffiti scribbled on the cell wall. I tried to imagine the boy entertaining himself, trying to hit a tin can or something like that with pebbles.

It was early one morning when they brought me here. The wind felt refreshing, and wrapped our chadors around our bodies. We had left the general ward blindfolded under guard. We were walking over hilly terrain. My toes were wet, picking up the moisture from the dewy grass.

"Rest a while," said the guard. "We've got a long way to go."

We were lined up close together, like peas in a pod. I could feel the guard standing next to me, and felt naked under his gaze. Intentionally, he blew his cigarette smoke in my face. "Let's get going," he said, as he stamped on his cigarette butt. "Lots of snakes here. Watch your steps." He chuckled. The air was redolent with the smell of grass crushed under our feet. From under the blindfold I could see the clay soil of the hills and small houses along the foothills with their rusted metal roofs reflecting the sun, which gave us a clue that the guard was marching us back and forth in front of those houses. We started grumbling. "All right. All right," he yelled. "Stop talking."

We then passed a low stone wall and entered an enclosure through a barbed-wire gate. We stopped when the guard ordered "Halt!" Some water squirted on my chador when I stepped on a loose brick.

"Here's a dozen beauties for you, Sister," the guard said teasingly to the female prison warden. We climbed up some stone steps.

—Did you just hire him?

—Forget about it.

—You son-of-a-bitch. Where do you find these good-looking kids, for god's sake?

—You're being a pest, you know? Your total for body work and paint is seventy tomans.

—Remember who you're talking to. I am flat broke until the end of the month.

The high-pitched voice of a woman rang in the fetid air of the big, half-empty hall, "Don't touch your blindfolds."

The smell of rotting tea leaves and kerosene made my stomach turn. I felt a sour taste in my mouth. I fought off an attack of diarrhea the best I could. I knew there wouldn't be a chance for a bath anytime soon.

The same female voice echoed in the hall again, this time sounding more masculine and authoritative, "Do not touch your blindfolds. Before you creep back in your holes, pay close attention to what I say." I caught sight of big cooking pots turned upside down to dry on the cement floor.

"Three meals a day," the woman shouted. "Morning, noon, and night. You must be ready in your cells to be taken to the washroom. There you do your business, wash your dishes, fill up your water jug, and do your ablutions." She paused briefly, wiggling her big toes in her bright orange slippers. "On the way back to your cell," she continued, "you pick up your meal and your tea. No foot-dragging.

No more than five minutes for anyone." And I hear the voice behind the prison wall:

—*Help yourself.*
—*Thanks a lot. Just leave it here. Needs a little more sand-papering, don't you think?*
—*As my brother says, tea must have a deep color. This looks like a baby's piss.*
—*Oh, come on. Don't be such a pain.*

"Make no mistakes," another female guard shouted from behind our line. She sounded as if she was chewing on something. "This is no grandma's house," she mumbled. "You can't knock on the door every time you have a headache or a pain in the butt." There was the sound of a metal drawer being shut forcefully. "Do you understand?" she went on. "Don't make a nuisance of yourself. If you have a serious problem, there is a piece of cardboard in your cell. Slide it under the door. Somebody will come and get you."

There was the clanging of heavy keys passed from hand to hand. We were ushered into our cells. The musty smell of paint was overpowering. I pulled the blindfold off my face. A shaft of sunlight from the barred window of the cell illuminated the graffiti on the wall. It occurred to me that regardless of the passage of time, I would never stop thinking about those who were here before me—imagining who they were, how they endured their time here, deciphering the words and images they left behind on these walls. I would visualize faces pale with fears, anguish, and hopes of "this too will pass," allowing my imagination to fancy secrets woven into the designs on the wall. Once I discovered a small ball of black hair stuffed into a tiny hole drilled into a cinderblock near the door, perhaps reminiscence of a belonging, a memory long past.

—*This is Radio Tehran. It is 9 a.m., dear listeners . . . Her image in my mind . . . Scent of flowers. . .*
—*Hey, boy. Leave that dial alone. They are all lies . . . How long . . .*

I slumped on the sack of clothes, exhausted. Something or someone, was being dragged on the floor in the corridor, and there was a hubbub of conversation. Suddenly I felt a tremor under foot. I heard the sound of a corrugated metal gate, like that of a store, being raised.

Gradually, the noise level behind the wall increased, and it included sounds like metal sheets or car fenders, being hammered, water being flushed from a garden hose, and the whine of an electric drill. There were many other noises I could not identify. They all filled my head in ceaseless vibration.

I spread a blanket on the cell floor and placed the water jug and plastic cup next to it. I wondered if I would go insane, but I was relieved to feel that the ambient noise was becoming increasingly routine and easier to get used

to as a natural component of the atmosphere of my existence, a lifeline letting me share in the lives of the people
beyond the walls of my cell.

Somewhere a door slammed hard, rattling the glass in
the window panes. A gruff male voice interrupted the hiss
of the paint sprayer.

—*Wait and See. I have plans for him, the SOB and . . .*
—*Don't take it too hard. He just made a mistake. . .*
—*Hey, boy, bring the paint. And a rag . . .*
—*Don't go overboard. Give me a call . . .*
—*Sure enough. Fifty tomans now. The whole invoice is
  seventy tomans; that's fair.*
—*How generous!*
—*Tell Zaghi this: Farmoon said not to get tangled with
  him . . .*

The sound of men laughing. Clicking of some keys,
perhaps being swung around on a keychain. A car door
slammed shut. The sound of tires on an unpaved road.

—*Ouch! Ouch! My hand. . .*
—*That'll teach you. Right?*
—*[silence]*
—*Don't let me catch you again talking to any jackass.
  Understood?*
—*Yes, yes. But he started talking to me . . .*

At sundown, before the guard, who I had nicknamed "Orange Slippers," locked the cell door on me, she said, "You look no more than fourteen to me."

"Fifteen," I responded.

"What a waste!" she said as she shook her head.

I put the plate and the water jug on the floor of the cell. I heard no sounds from beyond the wall or anywhere else, except the usual night sounds accompanied with the howling of a blizzard moving into the area.

Mother had brought with her some food and considerable anxiety. "There must be a mistake," she said emphatically. "My kid has nothing to do with politics! No way, what nonsense!"

My heart was racing, and not because of concern for the imminent physics exam at school. One of the two security agents showed Mother the warrant with my picture on it. Obviously, her pleas not to execute the warrant because I had to take an exam at school the next day would not go anywhere.

Books and papers were strewn all over the floor of the adjoining room. My botany project sat on a piece of cardboard, unfinished. I knew that my absence the next day in the biology class would not be considered excused. I had an acute awareness that it was not time for such thoughts.

Mother held my wrist firmly in one hand and with the other made gestures to the agents. "Remember, you said she'd be released tonight," she said, as we descended the dimly lit stairway to the door. "I will curse you if it turns out to be a lie." From the back window of the patrol car I saw her running, mouth open, waving my gray, hooded overcoat.

There was a layer of grease congealed on the surface of the soup, and no steam rising from the teacup. The tea had a chemical taste. I looked intently at the graffiti scratched on the wall. The words did not seem to have the same meaning as they did the day before. Even my emotions had altered in intensity and pattern.

I laid my head on the clothes bag and stretched my legs. They touched the opposite wall and made me feel claustrophobic. I was startled by the sudden barking of a pack of stray dogs. I spilled what was left of the tea in the cup. I smelled the stench of the wet wool rising from the blanket. As I drifted off to sleep, I wondered what set of thoughts would pass through my mind in the morning.

My days began with the noise of the corrugated iron gate of the shop being opened, followed by the plaintive singing voice of the young boy. I imagined him as being lanky, with an olive complexion. His lush black hair would cascade on his forehead and swing to the rhythm of the song: *I am a bird. I wish you were my mate in a cold, dark nest.* Perhaps his Adam's apple too moved up and down and his eyes glinted in the early morning sun. Intermittently, there was the sound of the older man clicking his tongue to the beat of the music.

—*Shall I break it? Didn't your mother teach you not to stand up to your elders?*
—*Ouch! Please, Boss. You are joking, aren't you?*
—*Done a good job with your hair.*
—*[silence]*
—*Don't be cheeky. Go get me the hammer, you punk kid.*

I was getting used to monotonous sounds of sanding and hammering. I stopped scratching the wall with the handle of a spoon. On the third day Orange Slippers stopped by my cell. I felt she'd been keeping an eye on me for a while. "Why you hang your head down like a sick chicken?" she asked in an admonitory tone. I said nothing.

—*Boss, Come and see if the dent is fixed.*
—*Give me the hammer.*
—*Here . . .*
—*Oh, for goodness' sake. Is this filler putty or a baby's shit?*

Someone is playing with the radio dial, tuning in one station after another. I didn't know why the man with the gruff voice pestered the boy so much. I developed a dislike for him. But whatever he was, he was a part of life that went on behind the wall. They came in the morning and left at night. In between, they lived life's routine. I felt like an observer watching some cave-dwellers through an opening in the wall of the cavern. My own life had become immaterial to me, like a vaguely remembered dream in which a middle-aged woman ran after a car trying to give one of the occupants a gray-hooded overcoat. This woman was not my mother. I did not have a recollection of ever having a mother. She was a figment of my imagination.

The paint sprayer stopped. The man with the gruff voice issued some technical instructions to the boy, or at least that was what I presumed.

—*Leave that alone. The wife has made us eggplant stew. Wash you hands and turn on the burner.*
—*Why do you trip me up, Boss? You remember I nearly smashed my knee last time.*
—*You're so damn slow. Get a move on.*
— *[silence]*
—*What do you think? Red or blue?*
—*Blue looks better, Boss, I told you so.*
—*All right, all right. Enough of that.*
—*I'm going to the stadium tomorrow.*

The man with the gravelly voice chuckled loudly. He started drumming on the hood of a car and with a falsetto began singing the lyrics of a racy and suggestive song.

In the corridor a trolley was being pushed along, serving food from cell to cell. A line of sugar ants extended from the floor all the way up the wall to where the light fixture held a low-wattage bulb in a wire cage. With my finger I crushed the ants leaving a trace of brown line on the whitewashed wall.

Suddenly, there was the sound of breaking glass and running feet. I pressed my ear against the wall.

—*I'm gonna beat the hell out of you bastard. Come back here.*
—*Oh, for god's sake, Boss. Please, I am only trying here . . .*
—*Shut the hell up! You take care of everybody except me.*
— *[silence]*
—*Come back. I just want to have a word with you, talk some sense into you.*

The bright afternoon sun had almost set and the breeze carried the smell of steel and paint. My knees were shaking.

A MAN AT the end of the alley, the alley near the school, caught me by surprise. I was trembling. With stretched arms, he advanced toward me. "I'm not going to hurt you," he said. "Just give me those." I stepped away from him. "These bastards," he shouted loudly. "They stop at nothing." Some neighbors looked on from their windows, some standing in doorways. I let drop the spray paint can and the brush. The hammer-and-sickle emblem on the white wall bled paint, losing shape.

"Look at what the bitch has painted on the wall," the man shouted at the onlookers, as he came close enough to me to feel his breath on the back of my neck. I broke into a run, the unbuttoned collar of my dress flapping in the wind. I burst into the stationary shop a few doors down from the school. The sales clerk looked up, startled. He pointed to the back door, wordlessly. The smell of books and newsprint filled my nostrils.

. . . The sound of water filling a bucket. The screech of metal grating against metal. The man with the raspy voice grumbled.

—*The son-of-a-bitch didn't take out the dent. He just filled it with putty.*
—*Sorry. I got distracted . . .*
—*Where the hell is the body mold? Not this one, the round-headed one . . .*
—*But Boss, this doesn't fit.*
—*What do you mean "doesn't fit?" Just watch.*

I couldn't laugh. Unaccountably, I thought of the story of the princess who draped her long tresses down the castle wall for her lover to climb up and rescue her from prison.

—*Jump up. I'll drop you off at the highway.*

Perhaps he leaped over an obstacle, or a tree branch snapped. I listened to the puttering sound of the motorcycle until it faded in the distance. I had a feeling that Orange Slippers has been watching me. I raised myself on my knees and looked toward the cell door. I heard the shuffling of the slippers moving away. The nightly howl of stray dogs had begun.

The repair shop opened later than usual. The man with gravelly voice cleared his throat. His grumbling was more bitter than usual.

—How dare you stand me up, you son-of-a bitch?

Sunlight had spread to the top of the wall. Pacing the cell for so long had made me dizzy. I stumbled to the floor. The ceiling seemed to turn round and round overhead pressing down on me. My breath was rapid and shallow. I tried to remember the poem I had written for my fellow inmates in the other cell block. No use.

The sound of a car pulling up to the shop door with tires skidding. The voice was high-pitched and sharp-toned, associated with men of small stature. It could be heard over the surrounding noises.

—Tailors have a reputation for being late. You make them look good, Farmoon.
—I swear I've been shorthanded, Mr. Tabesh. All is left is the polish, I swear.
—You can't lay up a government vehicle.
—I swear to all three of you gentlemen, I'll get it ready by tomorrow afternoon.

The sound of men talking casually among themselves and a car being driven away on a dirt road. A radio blaring in the shop.

—*Good morning, Boss.*

Something metallic was hurled. It crashed into a stone wall, making a ringing sound. Disgruntled mumbling of the man with the gruff voice.

—*How do you think it makes me feel to be stood up by a rotten kid? You think this is a game?*
—*Please don't beat me, Boss. . . I overslept . . . I swear on my mother's . . .*

Her hands at her waist, Orange Slippers was standing in front of my cell door swinging the oversized key ring. She had a twisted smile on her lips.

"Where are you?" she asked. "Do you have any aches and pains anywhere?"

The smell of cooked rice and minced meat stew with split peas was everywhere. The water jug slipped out of my hand and crashed on the floor in front of the washbasin. A narrow stream of dark yellow urine flowed on the mosaic floor. Orange Slippers jumped back. "That's precious," she said, her voice heavy with sarcasm. "You couldn't hold your piss for four hours. What the hell you thought you could do for the masses?"

Tuesday Prayer was being broadcast from the loud-speakers throughout the building. I rubbed the mirror with the palm of my hand and looked into it. My eye-lashes were clumped together with dry foam. There were pimples on my face. I had a strong desire to be alone by myself.

"Don't let that bother you too much," Orange Slippers said in a more conciliatory tone as she patted me on the back. "I'll take care of this. Tomorrow is bath day. Have your clothes ready." She then handed me the food plate and left another water jug on the floor and locked the cell door behind her.

I found the din of hammering and filing irritating. I removed the overcooked dried limes and split peas from the soup bowl.

"Every two or three months your father would sneak in for a visit," my mother had told me, "looking older and more decrepit than the time before. The signal was three rings on the phone after nine o'clock at night. I would raise the corner of the curtain of the parlor window to signal that the coast was clear.

"I would take a quick shower and cook his favorite minced meat stew. He was on the run and never stayed more than one night at a time. He often smelled musty and smoky. I could not sleep, afraid they would raid the house to catch him. He was always optimistic that things would get better with people rising and demanding their rights. I could not make him understand that people would not rise because he told them to." She then smiled and rubbed the the bulging veins on her hands.

"You were two years old," my mother continued, "as playful as a monkey, like you still are. You would hug his legs and he would lift you off the ground and swing you side to side. That made you laugh and laugh. Sometimes he sounded like he'd lost his mind. He said he would make you a swing from one end of the world to the other. Ultimately it was from a swing like that that they hanged him. I'd never know what kind of argument had persuaded him to think and act like that." She then stared at me with bloodshot eyes. "It looks like you are following in his footsteps," she moaned.

The hinges of the door of the shop squeaked. The man cleared his throat and spat. The crunch of his work boots on the sandy floor made the hair on the back of my neck stand on end.

—*Don't be scared, boy. Sometimes the devil gets under your skin.*
— *[silence]*
—*In this day and age you need sometone to take care of you. Or they'll stick it up your ass.*
—*[silence]*
—*Me? You see me here? I am in place of your dad. Why do you clam up?*

—*I don't know. What am I supposed to say?*

—*You don't have to say anything. Just treat me as well as you treat others.*

—*Leave me alone, Boss.*

—*Now drink up to get a buzz on.*

—*But with one's dad? This is . . .*

—*Oh, come on! Men don't cry. Don't spoil our day. Why are you sweating on a cold day like this?*

—*[silence]*

—*That's all right. Don't think about it. Hit me in the face if it makes you feel better.*

—*[silence]*

—*Now, remember you didn't hit when you had a chance. By the way, Mr. Fart was here this morning and unloaded a whole bunch of insults on me. Go ahead and polish the Mercedes. I don't want to deal with him again.*

—*[silence]*

—*Are you starving? Say something. I'm going to stop by the house and pick up some lunch. We'll be lucky if this leftover garbage from prison does not give us erectile dysfunction.*

A motorcycle drove away and its engine noise died beyond the hills.

—*I'll be no man if I don't kill him, that motherfucker.*

There was a tremor in the boy's voice. He had been shouting and now, as he chopped wood, he talked to himself.

Again, I could smell the odor permeating the cell. I did not want to think of their quarrels. But there was something bothering the boy, something I could not see or hear.

I was awakened by the squeak of the window in the cell door. I felt lifeless as I stretched on the floor of my cell, like a broken statue afraid to move lest some parts of my body would fall off. I moved slowly, deliberately. My sobbing filled the cell. I bit hard on the edge of the blanket. The salty taste of the wool filled my mouth.

I had a sense the boy had infiltrated my dreams, but I didn't know how. Every time I woke up I looked around apprehensively, afraid that someone had peeked into my dreams.

—*Hey boy, what's the matter? Your eyes are like hot coals. Come and get your lunch. It is healthy and nutritious.*
—*[silence]*
—*You've gone on silent mode again? Coo coo coo!*
—*Leave me alone, Boss. I don't like it this way.*
—*Wow! We're so serious, aren't we? That's why I like you as I do my own kid.*
—*[silence]*
—*I am like the good cop. You know? To serve and protect? I'll be looking after you any way I can.*

—[silence]

—Now tell me. In all honesty, how many of you were on the Saveh highway?

—Saber and . . . with me . . . four of us.

—I know what bastards they are. In their company you'll soon be a druggie.

—[silence]

—You'll be safe if you follow your boss. With those guys? I don't know.

—No, Boss. They are not into illegal . . .

—You're such a simple kid. They'll pull the wool over your eyes. Anyway, put out the fire and let's go in.

There was the hiss of water thrown on fire.

A key turned in a lock. With a wool cardigan and a pair of long pants under my arm, I followed Orange Slippers to the washroom. The windows were steamed up, condensation running down the glass pane. My cheekbones were protruding and a black mole had appeared on my neck. I felt the bliss of warm water on my body when the stall door flung open. It was Orange Slippers. I slid to a corner and tried to cover myself with my hands. "Don't worry," she said. "It is no stranger. I brought you a fresh towel. Let me scrub your back . . ."

On the way back to the cell, I plugged some courage up to ask, "Can you get me a book or some newspapers?"

"No, dear," she said, with a chuckle, looking at me quizzically. "There may be a cost involved."

"By the way," she said, changing the subject, "your complexion has improved . . . such a pity."

"How about The Book of Prayers?" I persisted.

"No, I can't do it, dear," she replied. "Don't worry. I'll pray for you myself. But let me see."

I lay down on the blanket still relaxed and drowsy after the hot shower. I jumped up to my knees by a loud and piercing shout. I could not tell what direction it came from. I looked around, confused. The floor vibrated briefly, as if a huge boulder had fallen on it nearby. There was the shuffle of hurrying feet and an engine being cranked to a start, followed by the sound of water sprayed from a hose under pressure.

Someone was sobbing audibly on the other side of the wall, mixed with the crowing of a flock of rooks. The sobbing had now subsided to hiccupping. By now the sunlight had withdrawn from the wall of the cell. With the handle of a spoon I scraped on the wall the face of a woman with long braids reaching all the way to the floor. Meals were now being distributed to the cells along the corridor. Behind the wall someone was chopping wood.

—*Hey, boy, where is your boss?*
—*Who?*
—*What do you mean who? Your boss, Mr. Farmoon.*
—*Oh . . . he just left.*
—*Is the car ready?*
—*Wait. I'll go get the keys.*

—Tell your boss to come up to the supply office tomorrow.
—Yes. Yes, sir.
—Tell him Hamed said hello.

Orange Slippers placed two boiled eggs on my plate. "I'm going to put your name down today for visits," she said.

The skylight was darkened by billowing smoke. I had been there two weeks and this was the first time the boy stayed in the shop overnight. His singing depressed me. It made me feel like I had lost something precious.

The smell of smoke filled the air. The dry wood cracked as it burned. The howling of the stray dogs sounded different, more like growling. In the distance a loud whistle echoed in the air, as the shriek of a malignant spirit haunting the surrounding hills. My knees trembled and I felt hot around the ears. I was overcome by a vague fear.

It seemed as if the black smoke was licked away by the bright red and blue flames of a blazing fire. A dog barked as the shop door was lowered with a loud bang. There was the smell of burnt flesh. My eyes were burning and I had a bitter taste in my mouth. The wall felt hot to the touch. There was a commotion—wailing and cries of pain echoed along the corridor. I beat on the bars of the cell door with my fists. The fire howled like a wild beast. The vision of a lone woman, her mouth wide open, running toward me, was superimposed on a background of fire and smoke. I was standing alone on the cracked bricks, sweat running down my spine. I felt a cool breeze on my face.

BEHNAZ ALIPOUR GASKARI is an award-winning writer, and has published two short story collections, a children novel, and several articles. Her latest collection of stories, *Bemanad*, received the Mehregan Literary Award in 2010. She is a college professor and literary critic, and lives in Tehran.

Intercession

Mitra Davar

THERE IS A PIECE OF FABRIC in my handbag I can't bring myself to throw it away. There are other items in the bag that I am attached to such as books, papers, ballpoint pens, lipstick, sunscreen lotion, etc. And there are images fixed on my mind: a knife, for example, held in a horizontal position.

But it is this piece of printed fabric, with a green-and-black background, that I try to keep out of sight, hidden in my handbag. Sometimes I get preoccupied with news reports in the paper. But more than anything else I think of the printed pictures of dead bodies, some mutilated or with their entrails displayed in full color, and wonder if the world has an abiding interest in our innards! In one corner of the page there is a picture of the American president, giving speech, or deep in thought.

I wish I could write under different circumstance. Lately I have been getting headaches every time I try to write. I just want to abandon all my belonging, even the contents of my handbag, and go get lost somewhere. I wonder how I can erase myself physically. There must be a tool for that purpose that operates smoothly. Qazaleh Alizadeh[1] did not choose the right way: hanging herself! It would have been better if she had taken some pills, or used gas, like Sadeq Hedayat.[2] Although, on second thought, that would not have been a good way either, what with all the gas molecules . . . nasty smell . . . asphyxiation.

A writer, poet, or novelist, must choose a way of dying worthy of his or her craft, such as food poisoning, followed by severe diarrhea and vomiting, then go to an isolated place in the mountains, lie down more or less in the direction of Mecca,[3] by observing the way anthills are lined up, and let his spirit rise from his body.

I don't know why I write about death and dying. Perhaps it is because these nights coincide with the mourning ceremonies for the Imam Hussein's martyrdom.[4] These past few nights we have been out joining the mourning processions. My parents and my husband Afshin prefer to stand in the doorway and watch. But my kids drag me into the crowds in the middle of the street.

The passage of time fourteen centuries later has not

[1] A popular Iranian poet and fiction writer (1947–1996). She committed suicide.
[2] A prominent Iranian writer (1903–1951). He committed suicide in Paris, France.
[3] In the Muslim liturgy, prayers and other spiritually significant events are undertaken facing Mecca.
[4] The anniversary of the death of Hussein ibn Ali (626–680), the third imam in the Shi'ite tradition and the Prophet's grandson, who died at the hands of his adversaries in the Battle of Karbala in today's Iraq, is observed widely and elaborately in Iran and among the Shi'ite community in other Muslim countries with mourning processions and ceremonies.

detracted our people from the imam's image as a martyr, or the public's longings for the righteousness of his cause.

A man shouts into a microphone of an enormous bull-horn, "Righteous!"

"O Hussein!" the crowd responds.

"Martyr!"

"O Hussein!"

The chant goes on to the deafening beat of drums and cymbals. The street is all lit up with colorful fluorescent lights. There is offering of sherbet and other refreshments. People are dressed from head to toe in black, weeping, moaning, and pounding their chests as an expression of grief. I notice two young men in black T-shirts and khaki pants. They have long, shoulder-length hair and as they move their heads in trancelike motions, the thick gold chains around their necks catch the eye. One of them executes elaborate footwork in time with the beat of the drum. I cannot take my eyes off the gold chains. My children watch them in open-mouth wonder.

All kinds of banners proclaiming religious slogans or displaying verses from the scripture are carried on the shoulders of men. They are decorated with peacock feathers and other types of ornaments and religious symbols. A woman covered in a black chador is standing next to a large and highly ornate banner. She is trying to tie a piece of fabric to it as a memento and an expression of her devotion. I listen intently as she whispers to the pole that upholds the banner. I can't hear a word.

The street reverberates to the roar of the crowd, chanting as prompted by the man with the bullhorn.

"Righteous!"

"Hussein!"

"Oppressed!"

"Hussein!"

"Martyr!"

"Hussein!"

A thin man, pulling a young calf with a rope around its neck, appears on the edge of the crowd and works his way to the middle of the street. The animal, eyes bulging, resists the move. A woman carrying a child emerges from the cabin of a pick-up truck parked at the curb.

"People," she screams, trying to raise her voice above the din. "I had vowed the sacrifice of a calf every year on this sacred day if God gave me a son."

She raises the baby for all to see and waves at the calf, as it is pulled laboriously to the middle of the crowd by the scrawny man. The animal looks around and stares for a moment at the carcasses of slaughtered sheep in front of the banner. After a moment's hesitation, it bolts. The thin man is dragged on the ground before letting go of the rope.

Some men run after the calf, which jumps wildly and frantically into the crowd, disappearing from sight.

A middle-aged man tries to draw away the attention of the crowd from the incident. He begins to flog himself rhythmically on his back with some lengths of chain attached to a wooden handle. In a booming voice he recites fragments from the Shi'ite book of common prayer.

"Thou art the beginning; thou art the end; thou art the hidden; thou art the apparent."

The words, glorifying God, are in Arabic, but they are familiar to the throngs of pious mourners.

They respond thunderously, fervently, and in unison, *"Ya man huwa!"*[5]

"Thou art the hidden; thou art the apparent. Thou art the first; thou art the last"

"Ya man huwa! Ya man huwa!"

The sound level reverberates through my body and makes my head ache. I squat down next to a tree, pressing my head in my hands.

I REMEMBER the time when I was in love. Sixteen years after the end of the war[6] they found his body, wrapped it in the national flag and shipped it to a holy site for burial. I read about it in the obituary section of the paper. I could not show up for the memorial service. How could I explain my presence there? I could not even see him when he was alive. I only knew he was there, and that gave me a warm feeling.

[5] "He Who Is!"
[6] A reference to the Iran-Iraq War (1980–1988).

I AM NOW past my prime, you might say. The skin on my face is sagging and shows signs of aging. I am getting old, slowly and inexorably. My children look so grown-up. I can see them in the crowds of mourners. Nima is in the circle of men, beating himself on the back with the chains. Bita and Behnaz, their eyes brimming with wonder, are in the women's section.

"Mother," Bita calls from a distance, "We've got you some cinnamon rice pudding."[7]

I push my way through the crowd, reach out, and hold the rice dish in my hands. A woman standing next to me exclaims in amazement, "Look, all the names of the Holy Five[8] appear on it!"

On the cracked surface of the pudding I see something like "Allah" traced in cinnamon.

"Say a prayer," a woman whispers in my ear.

Several other women stare at the pudding in amazement.

"Why don't you have some, Mom?" Bita asks. "You love the stuff."

"What a great man was Imam Hussein!" Behnaz proclaims. "He will still be great in several thousand years."

"Why don't you eat?" Bita asks again.

---

[7] A traditional dish distributed to mourners by religious organizations and charities. Often the names of imams and other holy persons are traced on the surface of the pudding in finely ground cinnamon.

[8] The Prophet, his daughter Fatima, his son-in-law Ali, and their two sons Hassan and Hussein.

By now the procession has started moving. The walls and storefronts along the street are covered with lengths of black fabric. I follow the procession and walk along with the crowds, trying to keep track of my children. I don't see Nima. The girls are indistinguishable among the women as they all look the same from behind: long black overcoats, black headscarves, black shoes, black pants.

A white sedan passes me by slowly. A small flag is attached to its side-view mirror. On it in red ink is inscribed "O, Fatima Zahra."[9]

"Nima!" I shout at the top of my voice to get the attention of my son, to no avail.

THE BLOODSTAINED carcasses of the sheep are dragged into a stately home with its front door wide open to a spacious courtyard where a large cauldron on a makeshift fireplace is bubbling over with boiling water.

"Marjan," my husband calls me from where he is standing near the doorway of a store.

I drop the bowl of rice pudding.

He calls to the children. Nima comes over. He points to a small cot in a corner of the yard. "That is Ali Asghar's[10] crib," he announces excitedly.

I break out in a sweat. Bita points to a quaint-looking

---

[9] The daughter of the Prophet and the mother of Imam Hussein.
[10] Imam Hussein's infant son. He was also a casualty in the Battle of Karbala.

old man with very long hair. "Look Mom," she say, "that is a dervish."

Bite-size wraps of grilled minced meat and herbs are now being passed around among those in the procession.

From the upper floor of a house with darkened windows a haunting chant can be heard,

"Every breath is of Ali, Ali."[11]

"Giver of breath is Ali, Ali."

An old man has managed to draw to him the attention of some men and women in the procession. "This is nothing," he is telling his audience. "In my youth there were mourner who beat themselves so hard that Imam Ali intervened to restrain them. Now the authorities don't let them do that. In those days they used long knives and machetes to slit their scalp and forehead. Blood everywhere. Some of them actually saw Ali. I never had the privilege. But I knew some guys who did."

Afshin grabs my hand and draws me toward our house. "I told you not to look at the slaughtered sheep," he admonishes me. "Remember how you collapsed when you came back from the pilgrimage to Mecca?"[12]

Now camels were being prepared for slaughter.

"Camels have a sense of what is going to happen to them," Afshin observes. "Many of them actually cry."

[11] The reference is to Ali ibn Abitalib, the Prophet's cousin, son-in-law, the fourth of the Rashidin Caliphs, and the first imam in the Shi'ite tradition.
[12] It is customary to slaughter sheep or goats upon the return of Mecca pilgrims to their dwellings.

There are rows of blood-soaked carcasses of slaughtered camels and sheep along the path of the slow-moving procession. I see the calf that had managed to get away earlier, now bound and ready for slaughter.

"You are so feeble-hearted," my father once said, "when it comes to the sight of blood or butchered animals. I knew a man named Zolfaghar Khan, who claimed to rip out the liver of a live sheep and eat it raw."

I was standing next to a brook, sweating profusely, and remember my mother who said that I was probably pregnant. "God willing," she said, "it's a boy. And if it is, I vow to sacrifice a sheep for Imam Hussein every year. I'll dress the child in black and take him to the mourning procession." And so here we are years later, mourning Hussein and coming to watch the ceremony of his martyrdom year after year.

I DON'T KNOW what I want to write about. I am holding that wrinkled piece of fabric in my fist. There was another funeral procession this morning. It was for those who had gone on pilgrimage to Karbala after the fall of Saddam Hussein and had been killed in a religious clash. Some family friends who returned alive brought us this piece of consecrated cloth—it had an association, however tenuous, with the Imam Hussein.

I don't know if the dead remain alive by themselves, or are kept alive by the living. The important thing is that they continue to stick around—all these images, pictures, sounds, daily funerals. And this piece of fabric brought to me as a souvenir.

They seem to be with us forever and ever . . .

MITRA DAVAR is a writer and essayist, and the author of short story collection, *Ya Man Huwa*, published in Tehran in 2005.

A Bloody Day of Ashura

Masih Alinejad

THE WORD IS THAT Ferdowsi Square is now occupied by "riot-control personnel." I park the Peugeot sedan near the overpass just before the intersection of two major boulevards and turn off the heater.

"What are we going to do now, Doc?" I ask the doctor, who is sitting next to me and has been as quiet as ever. Mahtab and Arash are in the back seat and have not exchanged a word since we left the house. Earlier in the morning they had had a long argument about taking part in the demonstration. A loose agreement had been reached to join the marchers by simply following them in the car.

Arash breaks up the awkward silence as he announces, "I'm going to get off." He wipes the steam off the passenger-side window of the car and peers outside.

"But the condition was that we all stay in the car and not join the crowds," objects his mother Mahtab, trying to tone down the emotion in her voice. Clearly, she does not want a repeat of the quarrel last night in front of the doctor, a perfect stranger.

The chilly blast of air feels good on my flushed cheeks as Arash cracks open the car door. "Yes, Mother," he says, stepping out of the car. "You made the decision, but I didn't say that I accepted it. I still feel bitter about your forcing me to stay home away from last December's demonstrations."

Now the doctor opens the door on his side, in an effort to ease the rising tension. Mahtab rolls down the window and pokes her head out. Her breath steams up in the chilly air as she addresses Arash, who has now crossed the curb and is standing on the sidewalk.

"So you want me to stay by myself in the car?" she asks, reproachfully. "I had a bad dream last night."

"You'll be all right in the car," Arash responds, heading toward Revolution Avenue. "We'll be back soon. Besides, you always have bad dreams."

I turn off the engine and eye Mahtab in the rearview mirror. She is gazing at the riot-control police lining the street. The look of anxiety is unmistakable on her face.

"You can take the car and go back home," I tell her. She has her hands pressed on her chest and doesn't respond.

"I'll leave the keys in the ignition," I continue. "It's up to you. Arash is right. You'll be safe in the car. But I *am* scared of your dreams," I add sarcastically, in a failed attempt at humor, and join Arash and the doctor heading toward the rally. It is sunny but cold.

I can't help but notice that the municipality has removed all the garbage cans and trash repositories. They were the first to be set on fire in demonstrations to generate smoke to counter the effect of tear gas in canisters lobbed by the police into the crowds. The state TV and media never report antigovernment demonstrations, but the dark spots on the asphalt left by the burning garbage pails tell the people where political rallies have taken place. For a while the municipality replaced plastic containers with metal ones. This time demonstrators not only burned the trash in them for smoke, but also used them as barricades against the advancing police columns. Now the municipality collects all trash receptacles in advance of a demonstration. Ironically, this tells people where and when a demonstration is planned to take place.

A massive crowd stretched for miles. I can hear them shouting in unison, "This month is the month of blood/ Washing away the tyrant in a flood."[1]

I continue to worry and feel concerned for Mahtab, hoping she would be scared enough to drive herself home.

---

[1] In December 2009, during the holy day of Ashura, there were several demonstrations in the streets of Tehran, and other cities in Iran, against the Islamic regime. These demonstrations ended in bloody confrontation, and the rounding up and jailing of hundreds of the protestors.

I see no sign of riot police as the crowds marches on. They are now more intense and animated. A new slogan fills the air, "Khamenei[2] is Yazeed,[3]/Both in word and in deed."

The pace of the procession slows as it approaches the intersection of Vali Asr. I hold the doctor by the arm and drag him along.

Earlier this morning I got a call from my mother. She tried every maternal appeal to prevent me from joining the demonstration. "Listen, Mom," I said sobbingly, "nearly a hundred of my friends and acquaintances are in jail. How can I stay home and not join the protest rally under the circumstances?"

The intersection of the boulevards is the designated end of the march. It is here that government forces, armed with firearms, nightsticks, and cattle prods are waiting, The formation suggests they are ready to charge the demonstrators.

Finally, the doctor ventures a remark, "We have been encircled, and if the police units assembled in the Ferdowsi

[2] Seyyed Ali Khamenei (b. 1939), currently the "Supreme Leader" of the Islamic Republic of Iran. Following Ayatollah Rouhollah Khomeini's death in 1989, Khamenei replaced him as God's Regent on Earth and was declared the Supreme Leader of the regime.

[3] Yazeed Ibn Mu'awiya (647–683) was challenged in his claim to the caliphate by Hussein Ibn Ali, the Prophet's grandson and the son of Ali Ibn Abitalib, the fourth of the Rashedin caliphs and the spiritual leader of the Shi'ite movement. In the ensuing hostilities culminating in the Battle of Karbala (May 680), Hussein was killed and thus reached the status of a martyr among the Shi'ites, who consider Yazeed his murderer and the arch-villain in the conflict.

Square attack from behind," he says contemplatively, "we would all be trapped with no escape route to get away."

He is right. I feel depressed at the prospect of being detained and interrogated again. Arash, who is behind us in the press of demonstrators, grabs the doctor by the arm and places himself ahead of us. He slows the pace of our contingent apparently in preparation for disengaging from the crowd. Obviously, he too is concerned about Mahtab and knows that being arrested at this point would be disastrous for all of us. But the people are still pushing forward, making it harder for us to withdraw. The slogans are increasingly belligerent—and deafening: "Death be to the oppressor / Be it the Shah or the confessor."[4]

We have now been carried by wave after wave of demonstrators to the pedestrian crossover bridge near the major intersection. "He who claims to be just," the marchers shout, "has betrayed the nation's trust." Involuntarily we join in the chorus.

Suddenly, the street is rocked by the sound of firearms. Somehow, at the sound the marchers become more cohesive and nuanced in their advance. "Have no fear, have no fear," they chant, "We are together now, and here!" This is the slogan shouted in demonstrations to boost morale in face of danger.

---

[4] The references here are, respectively, to Shah Mohammad Reza Pahlavi, the last ruling monarch of Iran, deposed in 1979, and the current Supreme Leader, Ali Khamenei.

Below the overhead bridge there are piles of sandbags. The municipality keeps them along major thoroughfares for snowy days. Now protestors are using them as a barricade to prevents the motorcycle police commandos from running down the demonstrators. But some bikers and members of the Basij militia[5] have infiltrated the march, clashing with demonstrators in fist fights with the crowd.

"Let us cross at the bridge," Arash yells at us over the din. "Mahtab may be scared to death sitting in the car."

I am thinking along the same lines. But it is impossible to penetrate the crowd and too dangerous to cross the street where rocks are being hurled in all directions.

"Oh my God!" the doctor yells and lets go of my hand.

"What's the matter, Doc?" I ask, alarmed. He raises his hand and points to the top of the bridge where two young Basijis are leaning on the banister looking down.

"Those bastards!" the doctor exclaims, pointing at them. "They threw somebody off the bridge."

I feel hot and sweaty, despite the freezing air, and rush toward the scene, followed by the doctor and Arash. We can't get close because of the crowds.

"He's still alive," someone yells from the front rows of the bystanders.

Arash, taller than average and now standing on tiptoes, has a commanding view of the scene. "He's alive,"

[5] Basij is a loosely organized paramilitary militia maintained by clerics in the Islamic regime. Units of the organization are deployed against demonstrations and activities of the opposition.

— 124 —

he announces. "His face is covered with blood. They are taking him on a motorbike."

The news of the Basiji atrocity reaches the ranks of the marchers. Those nearby look around trees, hedges, empty lots for rocks or anything that can be thrown at the perpetrators.

"Friends, keep your cool," Arash shouts at the top of his voice, which has an impressive range. "Control yourselves. The Basijis want to provoke us."

I pull at his arm in an effort to prevent him from making a scene. "This is a conspiracy," he shouts again. "Don't fall for it. We are all Greens. Our movement is nonviolent."[6]

"That's enough," I hiss at Arash. "Calm down, for goodness' sake."

The crowds are now in a state of frenzied rage, throwing anything they get their hands on at the Basijis, who find their position untenable and begin to retreat. Half a dozen of them abandon their motorcycles and run toward an old building, apparently a government office, but before they can reach it they are overtaken by the crowd and bitten. They raise their hands over their head for protection against the attack and rain of rocks and other projectiles.

Arash pulls himself out of our clutch and elbows his

---

[6] The protesters against the declared outcome of the 2009 presidential election in Iran were designated as "Greens," partially due to a reference by founder and former presidential candidate Mir Hussein Mousavi, calling the movement the "Green Path of Hope" as a nonviolent civil rights movement.

way through the crowd to where the Basijis are cowering in a doorway. He stands in front of them and spreads his arms.

"Stop it, brothers. Stop it," he bellows. "I swear you to what is sacred . . ." A rock hits him on the forehead before he can finish his sentence. He wobbles briefly and collapses to the ground. I pull my hand out of the doctor's grip and run toward him. I can only hear my own scream. Two older women rush to my assistance. Rock throwing ceases. From the corner of my eye I can see a crowd of demonstrators punching and kicking the cornered Basijis, who have now been divested of their helmets and Kevlar vests. The smell of burnt rubber is overpowering.

I help Arash stand up. But when I try to pull him away with me, he resists and stumbles to where the Basijis are being bitten by the crowds. He reaches a young Basiji and lifts him into his arms, holding his bloodied head to his own chest. I can hear myself shrieking as some punches make contact with his face.

I can feel the heat of flames behind me. I look back and I see the riot police motorcycles on fire in a pile.

Two other women approach me to help Arash. I can see some people with their cell phones raised above the crowd shooting pictures and videos.

The young Basiji has now surrendered himself to Arash, who is bleeding from a gash on his forehead. One eye is shut with coagulated blood, the other raised skyward, streaming with tears. Blood sprays from his nose with every breath. The surrounding crowd is calmer now. More people come forward to help, most of them women of all ages. I desperately look for the doctor.

Now that the crowd has calmed down, Arash lets go of the Basiji's head. He tucks the young man's hand under his arm and leads him to the sidewalk where they both slump on the curb. The sight of the Basiji's face covered in blood turns my stomach. I can't bear to look at the swelling where his eyebrows were and the tear at the corner of his lip from which a trickle of blood drips down his chin.

The doctor now appears, carrying a bottle of mineral water. He uncaps the bottle and tries to pour the water on Arash's face. But Arash grabs the bottle in mid-air.

"Cold water helps stop the bleeding," the doctor grunts.

Arash wrests the bottle from the doctor's grip and splashes some water on the Basiji's face. Blood washes down his face through his beard and drips on the ground between his legs. He then takes a swig from the bottle, gurgles the water in his mouth, and spits out some thick, red liquid. I almost vomit.

Arash rises and helps the young man to stand up. They start walking toward the intersection. The doctor and I follow them. The wind spreads heavy smoke in all directions. I can hear the crowd cheering. The government building is now engulfed in flames.

People are still throwing rocks at the contingents of riot police lined up along the boulevard. They stop when they see us moving in that direction. We walk past a crowd of irate Greens. They stop their rock-throwing barrage, watching us intently. At a short distance from the police lines Arash stops. The Basiji, without looking back, moves toward his colleagues and disappears in their formation. I help Arash to get back to the ranks of the Greens.

According to reports, police patrol cars have ploughed into the crowds of Greens in the city square, killing several.

When we get back to overpass bridge, we find no sign of Mahtab or the Peugeot sedan.

MASIH ALINEJAD was a parliamentary reporter for major reformist newspapers, until her critical articles led to her dismissal in 2006. She now lives in England, and received a degree in communication from Oxford Brookes University. She has written *The Crown of Thorn* about her experience as a young journalist in Iran.

The Bathhouse

Shahla Zarlaki

THE HINGES OF THE corrugated iron door of the bathhouse squeak as it opens. No sooner have we crossed the
threshold than a thick, milky steam engulfs us. We are
greeted by a hubbub of unfamiliar voices—women talking,
laughing, children shrieking. Though only yards away, the
noise seems to be muffled by the denseness of the steam.
The sounds modulate in volume but not enough to drown
Mother's injunction: "Watch your step so you don't fall
again." She follows her mother's warning by scanning
the rotunda of the bathhouse, looking for a spot for us to
occupy. With every step I take I have the fear of slipping
on a slimy spot or the remnants of a bar of soap abandoned
on the floor. I hold the plastic bowl in front of my chest.

It never takes Mommy Ati any length of time to find
a vacant alcove for the three of us in the atrium of the
bathhouse, crowded with naked, boisterous female bathers. As usual, Fariba rushes ahead to access the fourth
shower, which she believes has more water pressure than
the others. Mommy Ati splashes some water on a spot

near the central pool in an effort to sanitize it for us to sit on. Before we are settled, the wife of Saj Ali, the local greengrocer, spots us from across the central pools. Her head is covered in soapsuds and she is rapidly blinking trying to keep it out of her eyes.

"Good morning, Mrs. Atieh. Good to see you." Her voice rings under the dome of the atrium, bringing unwanted attention to us. "Any more phone calls? Any news?" she wants to know. My mother responds dismissively, to let her know she is not particularly pleased with the encounter. "Having a telephone," she grumbled once," has made us the central news agency of the whole neighborhood."

MOMMY ATI places the heavy receiver of the black German-made telephone next to her on the carpet and turns to me. I know I have to set aside my doll on the bedroll and wrap myself in my chador that has flower patterns on a white background. "Run over to Saj Ali's store," she orders. "Tell him it is long distance."

I put on my foam-rubber slippers, still smelling new. They are yellow, the color of melted butter on breakfast toast. I run on the freshly paved asphalt across the alley to the store. As I run, my chador is lifted, making me feel like I'm flying in the air. I find it gratifying that our telephone brings news to us first; we are receivers of important, world-shaking news, and we dispense it to grateful neighbors and acquaintances. Mommy, too, cannot hide her amusement at the effusive expressions of Saj Ali's wife, "Dear, dear Mrs. Atieh! I am crazy about your telephone!"

"Hello? Hello? Is that you, Hojjat? Are you all right?" shouts Saj Ali, holding the receiver upside down to the side of his face.

I am standing by the door giggling. Mommy frowns at me as she reaches for the receiver. "Uncle Saj Ali, you're holding it wrong again," she says impatiently. "This way." Saj Ali, who is cross-eyed, looks sheepish as he presses the receiver to his ear. He hands the receiver to Mommy when the conversation ends and leaves the house, uncharacteristically without profuse expression of thanks. In the alley, he leans against a poplar tree looking skyward, the pupils of his eyes pointing in different directions. He does not offer me the customary snacks of nuts and raisins he always carries in his pocket. He mumbles something to a neighbor standing in the doorway.

Later, when father is watering the tree with a garden hose, I ask about Uncle Saj Ali. "Nothing for you to worry about, dear," he says. "Apparently his son is missing in action in the front."[1]

Also the news of the son of another neighbor, Haj Morteza, who volunteered to go to the front and is now suffering from shell shock, is delivered by our telephone.

[1] A reference to the Iran-Iraq War (1980–1988).

Fariba, always intent to get to the bottom of things, wants to know what that means.

"Shell shock, you know, combat stress," Mommy bursts out impatiently. "Must everything be translated for you? Don't you know anything?"

We have come to view our telephone like a capricious monster, perched on an elevated spot in the living room, dispensing good or bad news at will. Mommy sets the receiver next to her on the carpet and turns to me. Loathe to be the bearer of bad news, I try to ignore her by raising my geography textbook in front of my face, trying to memorize the name of the longest rivers in the world.

I AM STILL trying to squeeze myself between Fariba and a neighboring lady in the alcove. Mommy pours a bowl of hot water over my head. I let out a squeal. "These old hags!" she complains. "They overheat the water. I am surprised their skin doesn't peel off."

In my constricted space, I rest my chin on my knees and watch Mother washing Fariba's hair as I wait for my turn. Her unhurried pace tells me we are going to be here for a while yet. She takes the bathing paraphernalia out of the plastic bag and arranges them next to the pool. She is fond of Golnar soap and Darougar shampoo. I hug my knees firmly. I realize that there is no sign of the woman I call the mermaid. She usually comes on midweek days when the place is less crowded. She always takes the alcove to the right of the second pool, near the exit door. First she kneels on her right knee, then lifts her right knee, balancing herself on her left hand as she turns her head over her shoulder. In doing so, her long black hair, still dry, streams down her back all the way to the crook of her narrow waist. In this pose, before she starts scraping her heel with the unsightly pumice, she reminds of the picture of a mermaid I once saw in a storybook.

Fariba is adroit and agile as she rubs the washcloth over her flat stomach and spindly legs, ignoring Mommy's advice not to expose kneecaps to too much moisture to avoid pruning. She is not embarrassed of her own body. I feel envious that she will soon be in the dressing area with her hair wrapped in a towel, while I will still be standing in a corner of the shower stall waiting for Mommy to go through the ablution ritual, enunciating the required chant, before attending to me. Fariba will be past the first intersection on the way home while Mommy meticulously rubs my entire body, like that of a newborn baby, with the soapy washcloth. By the time I am wrapped in the towel, still damp from Fariba's hair, she is halfway home, loosening the knot of her silken headscarf to allow a curl of her hair to dangle on her forehead for the benefit of Haj Morteza's son, who is watching from the window of the carpet shop.

Fariba always refers to the last shower stall in the bathhouse the old ladies' chamber. It is infused with the smell of old plaster mixed with that of depilation compound.

She says there is a secret behind the foul odor emanating from the drainpipe, but she doesn't share it with me. She raises her plucked eyebrows and looks at me condescendingly. She is not aware that I have been peeping through the hole in the metal door and have my own stash of secrets.

"Why are you so dazed?" Mommy Ati howls at me. "Get a move on. Your feet are pruning."

"Possibly it is due to calcium deficiency," the woman with the close-cropped haircut observes, as she slides a silver-handled razor up her leg. "Some children are more prone to it than others. Look how her heels have puffed up."

I feel an irritation in my heels. If I were in the dressing area, Khavar Khanom, the manager on duty, would never miss a chance to comment on my puffy heels. I continue to imagine that when Khavar Khanom would ask for our locker number, which is twenty-four, I would be holding the large comb in front of me as a gesture of modesty to hide those ridiculously small protrusions on my chest. She would rub a block of salt on my feet. The swelling goes away and wrinkles disappear. I would smell the stew Khavar Khanom is cooking on a burner in the corner of the dressing room. The cool, fresh air of the dressing room would relax me. I think of the freezing air on the street and the warmth of my ski jacket protecting me against it. If it weren't for those math problems waiting for me at home, I would be the happiest little girl in the world.

But for now I am squeezed between the warm fleshy thighs of my mother. She is wringing my hair, as she does laundry in a tub, with her thick fingers, dousing it with bowl after bowl of hot water to make sure all soap is washed out of it. I have my eyes closed in agony, points of light floating behind firmly pressed eyelids. My ears are covered by soapsuds, tiny bubbles bursting noisily, muffling the sounds around me.

Suddenly, I do not feel the touch of my mother's thighs and beyond the tiny explosions of soap bubbles I hear the rising howls of fear. I open my eyes. I see only darkness, as if the darkness behind my closed eyelids has now extended to the space before it. I see specter-like outlines of white bodies running helter-skelter in the dim light of the bathhouse. I crawl toward the pool and take refuge against its warm border wall. I know it is the bomb alert and the blackout will not last long. As on Friday three weeks ago, Khavar Khanom will open the door and yell over the noise of the bathers, "Ladies, it is situation red alert . . . Just wait a little while . . . They'll sound the all-clear siren shortly . . . It will be over in a minute."

Seconds pass slowly. Images become fainter in my eyes and the noise more distant. But some utterances pierce the hum and the sound of bursting soap bubbles in my ears.

"A woman is in labor . . . there's trouble . . . call emergency . . . only if she gets to the hospital fast . . . may God have mercy . . ." I think of tiny soap bubbles bursting in my head like a bomb exploding.

Khavar Khanom brings in an oil lamp and places it on a window ledge. The yellowish glow of the lamp dilutes the darkness. I now see that I am by myself and there is a gathering of ghostlike bodies around one spot near the entrance door. I walk in that direction past the second pool. Mommy Ati, her hands at her waist, is standing at the edge of the congregation next to the woman with the butch haircut talking to her. She is frowning, agitated. Now she sees me and is clearly upset.

"Where do you think you're going?" she yells at me. "Go sit down. You'll slip and fall."

I walk slowly and gingerly, to assure her of my safety. The women have gathered in a tight circle around something or someone I cannot see. I cannot penetrate the tangle of wet and naked bodies. I slide down to the floor. The first thing I see is the blond hair spread over the dark-brown mosaic floor. I won't go any further to see the face and the rest of her body. I know she is the same tall, attractive woman who caught my attention in our last visit to the bathhouse. I vaguely recall what the woman with close-cropped hair was saying about her as she applied the imported shampoo to her short hair: "She'd had an easy pregnancy . . . she must be due any day, but has no swelling . . . It doesn't look like she's had any morning sickness . . . I bet it's a boy."

I see the thin rivulet of blood flowing from under the woman's body to the drain cover. Over the din, I can only catch snatches of the conversation my mother is having with the short-haired woman.

"Victim of evil eye . . . some people have evil eye . . . they're jealous . . . envious."

The bomb has exploded at some distance from the bathhouse. With the soapsuds crackling in my ear, I may not have heard it. I can't stand here. My knees are shaking and I feel pins and needles in the soles of my pruning feet. I feel as if something malignant is growing inside of me. I straighten my back, standing at full height. I start walking toward the fourth shower stall which, according to Fariba, has the highest water pressure. On my way I notice Saj Ali's wife whimpering, cursing Saddam.[2] She is not trying to cover any part of her aging body. Somehow, I am amused. I swagger past her, walking as I think the blond woman, now sprawled on the floor, would walk. I feel secure and protected from public view in the semi-darkness of the bathhouse. I stand under the warm water spouting from the showerhead, imitating Mother's ablution ritual. The flow of warm water over my body feels heavenly. I have an urge to grab a razor and shave my legs to get rid of the pubescent fuzz, and the wrinkly knees that Mother likens to those of a camel. I think of grabbing the foul-smelling depilatory compound and smearing it all over my body to emerge white and spotless, like the pregnant woman now

[2] Saddam Hussein, the former president of Iraq.

lying under the gaze of inquisitive eyes. I have a new and resurgent spirit in me, joyous and unafraid of whatever life may throw my way, even of Saj Ali, covering my face with wet and toothless kisses every time I deliver messages from his son on the front.

I emerge from the shower stall. The all-clear siren has sounded. The lights are back on, and there is no sign of the blond woman on the floor near the exit door, except for spots of her congealed blood mixed with soapsuds. I see Mommy Ati looking around, desperately searching for me. I straighten my back and walk upright as I pass the blood-smeared discarded bits of soap on the floor.

SHAHLA ZARLAKI is a short story writer and essayist who lives in Tehran. Her short story collection, *We were Dinosaurs,* was published in Tehran in 2010.

The Wandering Cumulus Cloud

Zohreh Hakimi

THE SKYLARK HAS JUST LANDED on the wall and begun its tuneful chirp when the rain starts to fall. There is a knock on the door.

"Poor bird!" I lament. "The rain starts just as he begins to sing."

"Don't worry about the lark," says my mother. "Go open the door."

As I watch the bird, I move up the stairs to the entrance hall and open the door. I see Monir, and I'm taken aback by her appearance: she has a gash on her lower lip that extends down to her chin, her eyes puffy and red.

"Hello, Sis," I blurt out, not knowing what else to say.

She pushes her way past me as she enters the hall.

"Hello," she says perfunctorily. "Is Mother home?" she asks, some sharpness in her tone.

"Yes," I reply mechanically. "She is in the yard."

"Where's Father? Isn't he home?"

"No. I don't know where he is."

She crosses the hall and I follow her as she runs down

the stair to the yard. "Hi," she says to Mother, who is standing at the foot of the steps looking up, immobilized by Monir's appearance. Her glance moves from the gash on her lip to a large bruise on the side of her neck.

Monir drops the little sack she is carrying and sits on a step. She lowers her head to her knees and begins to sob. Mother opens her mouth in an effort to say something but she fails. Monir's sobbing echoes around the little yard.

"Oh my God," Mother finally exclaims. "Has it happened again?"

Monir's shoulders tremble as she sobs uncontrollably.

"For heaven's sake, child," Mother begs, "say something. I'm dying to know what happened."

Monir's crying is now a muffled scream. "Mother," she manages to articulate, "I am *not* going back to that house. If Father insists that I do, I swear to God I'll run away."

Mother looks at me as if saying, "Here we go again!" She sits on the step next to Monir putting an arm around her shoulder. "Tell me again what happened," she says.

"Just look at this," Monir retorts as she points to her face. "What do you think happened?" She then pushed her sleeves up and displays cuts and bruises covering her arms. I avert my eyes.

"That is how the rest of my body looks," Monir whimpers. "I can't bear this anymore, Mother." With the cut on her lip and a swollen jaw she has difficulty uttering a word.

Mother, in agony, bites her lip and slaps the side of her face. "Look at that," she exclaims. "May God break his arms!" It is only now that she notices the rain. "Let's go in," she says. "We're going to get wet."

"So I should expect to be beaten to death for Father to take pity on me?" Monir asks provocatively, as she gently touches her injured lip. "The first time you told me to go back to him and I did. This time you can't force me to go back.

"God help us all," says Mother, shaking her head.

Now the rain is coming down in sheets. The lark is still perched on the wall, soaking wet.

WE CAN HEAR Father in the yard clearing his throat noisily. Color drains from Monir's face. "Mother," she implores, "please tell him I can't live with Rasool anymore. He is crazy. Please do your best to convince him to get my divorce."

Father enters the room. "Hi," the three of us say in unison. He is taken aback at the sight of us, but instantaneously he looks at Monir. "What happened to your face, Sweetie?" he asks, more curious than concerned.

"Oh, nothing," Monir responds, evasively. "Mother will tell you."

He casts a searching glance around the room. "Are you by yourself?" he wants to know. "Rasool didn't come with you?"

Monir shakes her head. "He'll come later," she mumbles.

He strides across the room and goes to the balcony. Mother follows him there. Monir and I wait behind the door in anticipation of hearing their conversation. We can't hear what Mother says, but we hear Father loud and clear.

"That bastard had promised not to raise his hand on this kid," he bellowed.

Mother's response was too muted for us to understand, but he hisses vehemently enough for us to hear, "Don't make a big thing out of it. So what if he has given her a whack or two?"

Again, an inaudible comment from Mother.

"She's done the wrong thing. This spoiled kid packs a bag and comes over here at the slightest excuse."

Father is now positively yelling, "Who cares if she's got a few bruises? She's not dead, for heaven's sake. Does she tell us about when they're having their touchy-feely times together? So they should keep their arguments and rough times between themselves."

"Oh, for God's sake," we hear him burst out, "didn't I talk to him three months ago? Didn't he promise to behave himself? What if he turns around and says he'd divorce her? What could I say to that?"

We can only guess what Mother has said to get this reaction from Father: "The hell she has asked for divorce herself! Has she no consideration for family honor? I'm not going to blow our reputation over this giddy-headed girl. Tell her that if she mentions the word divorce again, I'll disown her. I swear to God."

"MY DEAR AUNTIE," Monir says earnestly, "I swear on the Koran I can't bear this anymore. What have I done to deserve a lifetime of indignation and abuse?"

Auntie extends her feet into the spot of sunlight streaming in from the window and inhales deeply on the hookah pipe in front of her. The passage of air through the water in the glass urn makes the green leaves in it dance wildly. A large wasp buzzes loudly behind the windowpane. She watches the wasp as she puffs on the hookah.

"He wouldn't beat you for no reason at all," Auntie says finally. "Perhaps you've disobeyed him in some way. Perhaps you've done something to set him off and make him see red."

"No, no," Monir insists, "I swear I never do anything wrong. He just gets up and starts beating on me for no reason at all. I swear he is crazy. Mother can tell you. All my body is black and blue." She then reaches for Auntie's hand and holds it between hers.

"Auntie," she pleads, "I beg of you, on your son's grave, tell Father to pursue my divorce."

Auntie pushes the hookah away abruptly and looks at Mother, frowning. "What is this girl talking about?" She asks, her voice laden with disapproval. "Who in our family has gotten a divorce for this to be the next?"

Mother lowers her head, clearly mortified. "I don't know. Just my bad luck."

Auntie now addresses Monir, glaring. "Shame on you! Suppose he's beaten you over the head a couple of times. What of it? That's not a reason to bring up talk of divorce." Turning to Mother, she continues, "What a way to raise children!" She hisses sarcastically. "Congratulations!" She goes on, "I have sent five daughters into marriage. You haven't heard a squeak from any of them. God knows what they have had to put up with so they wouldn't be called a divorcée."

For a long moment, Auntie stares at Monir. "I suppose," she says bitingly, "those poor girls now have to bear the shame of *your* divorce!"

THE SPICE SHOP of our elder brother is heavy with the aroma of myriad spices. We stand in a corner and wait for him to take care of some customers.

"Hello," I mutter, when the customers leave. Monir follows suit, somewhat hesitantly.

Big Brother acknowledges us, looking cool and distant.

"Father told me you're back again after a quarrel," he says without looking at us.

Monir nervously adjusts the chador on her head. "That's why I came to see you, Big Brother," she says in a tremulous voice. "Please talk to Father, I beg of you. Get him to file a complaint with the family court,[1] or give me permission to do it myself. Once Rasool sets foot in the court, everyone will see he is crazy."

Big Brother flushes, arteries in his neck throbbing visibly.

"If you've lost your mind, I haven't," he retorts. "I'm not that stupid to ask Father to get involved in that sort of thing. I suppose you mean ultimately to file for divorce."

Silent tears roll down Monir's face. "What if I do?" she says. "Is that God's will for me to put up with this lunatic for the rest of my life?"

She then pushes the chador off her head to expose the injuries on her face and neck. Big Brother briefly gazes at her. Something darkens in his eyes as he lowers his glance. "Goddamn!" he mutters.

"Her whole body looks like that, Big Brother," I venture. He looks at me as if he has just noticed my presence.

"Don't you have school and school work to do instead of getting involved in this?" he reproachfully asks.

"No school on weekends," I respond.

Big Brother reaches for a cigarette in the drawer of the desk in front of him. As he strikes a match to light it, his hands tremble so hard he has trouble holding the flame to the cigarette.

---

[1] A female plaintiff cannot initiate the divorce process on her own without the explicit consent of a male blood relative, unless the right to file for divorce is indicated in the marriage contract.

He points to a stool near the wall. "Take the weight off," he says to Monir, who is now crying openly. She balances herself on the stool.

"Goddamn!" hisses Big Brother under his breath, staring at the tiles on the floor, "He'd promised not to hurt her anymore."

"He started the next day after we made up," Monir whimpered. "He says he can't help it."

Big Brother puffs on his cigarette silently for a minute. "Well," he says, still looking down at the floor, "I know he has a temper. But you can't file for divorce whenever you're not having a good time at home. I suppose," he goes on, snickering, "if you get a divorce, my wife will follow suit. She'll fancy a divorce if I ask for a cup of tea. Things fall apart that way."

"Take my word for it," he says, as he throws the cigarette butt on the floor and steps on it, "It's best if you go back home before it is too late. Don't embarrass yourself more than you have already."

"OH, SWEETHEART," Grandma coos soothingly. "You make it sound like he's stabbed you with a sword."

The setting sun has now slid off the top branches of the locust tree and is shining on a bed of pansies near the bench where Grandma is sitting as she combs her hair.

"Grandma," Monir responds, "I swear to God, when he gets that way, he *will* run me through, if he could lay his hands on a sword. He's out of control, Grandma." She then pushes her stockings down for Grandma to see the bruises on her legs. She grimaces at the sight.

"Oh, my goodness," she wails, "look at my child's legs!" she then turns to Mother. "You should have put some ointment on them," she rebukes.

"All my body is like that," Monir adds. "I can't be covered in ointment all over."

"Look here, Grandma," Monir says tearfully, "Father listens to you more than he does to anyone. After all, you're his mother. He will not turn you down. Please tell him to file for my divorce, or at least give me permission to do it myself."

Grandma arranges the white scarf over her henna-dyed hair, and knots it under her chin.

"This kind of talk is inappropriate, sweetheart," she says in a sober tone. "In every relationship there is some conflict at first. Gradually you get used to each other. Nobody is perfect. Everybody has a flaw of some kind. His problem is his temper. On the other hand, he is faithful and doesn't have a roving eye. He is not into drugs or alcohol. Most likely, once he is a father, he'll change completely. If you want my advice, try to have a baby."

Monir listens silently, teardrops slowly rolling down her face. Grandma takes a deep breath and continues, "Besides, do you think I got better treatment from your late grandpa? You never heard a peep from me. I knew if I sued for divorce, that would embarrass the whole family."

MOTHER HAS SPREAD her sewing on the floor of the balcony. Monir sits down beside her. "What have I done to get everyone mad at me?" she asks, not really expecting an answer. "None of you could bear living a week with Rasool, getting a beating on a daily basis."

Mother spreads a skirt on her lap and begins hemming it. "Just think of our reputation, sweetheart. All this talk about divorce," she says with a deep sigh. "Do you really believe I want you to get hurt? My heart bleeds for you, I swear. But divorce is not the answer. At least there you have your own home and you are the lady of your own house. Well, you have a bad-tempered husband, but that is better than being divorced and cooped-up in the corner of this house."

"Why cooped up?" I blurted out, knowing full well I was risking Mother's fury. "She's only twenty. She could go to school and at least get her diploma."

"She's right Mother," Monir says, with a faint suggestion of a smile on her face. "I can go to school."

Mother clutches the fabric and rises to her feet as she gazes at me, eyes blazing. "You need not put words in her mouth," she says to me, wagging a finger. "She's already got enough wrong ideas in that head of hers."

"But what's wrong with the idea of going to school?" I persist, refusing to be intimidated.

"Oh, Shut your trap, you punk kid!" Mother yells. "If she comes back as a divorcée, not even a dog will look at this house for a bride, and then you too will rot here as an old maid!"

AFTER WE HAVE breakfast, Monir wraps herself in the chador. "Mother," she says, sounding resolute. "I'm going to do something about this situation myself today.

Mother looks at her, frowning. "Once you set foot in a police station or the family court—whatever—your father will never again let you in this house. I'm telling you so that you know he will not tolerate a dishonored daughter."

Monir sinks to her knees near the door and bursts out crying.

MONIR FILLS a glass with tea and places it on a tray. "I'll talk to Father myself," she announces. She draws a deep breath and heads for the yard, carrying the tea tray. I watch her from the open window.

Father is moving the flower pots from the greenhouse, arranging them by the wall for later planting in the flower beds. The air is infused with the fragrance of jasmine and carnation. A flock of sparrows chirps loudly in the honeysuckle bush growing up a tree. A white puff of cloud is drifting across the blue sky.

Monir places the tea tray near the small reflecting pool in the yard. "Father," she calls.

He places a large pot of blooming gardenia near the other pots and sits on the narrow ledge of the pool. Monir squats on the ground next to him and looks up directly into his face. He lowers his head, avoiding eye contact with Monir, who cracks her finger joints and seems hesitant. "I want to talk to you, Father," she finally says.

"I have nothing to say to a daughter who doesn't care about her father's reputation," says Father, his eyes closed.

"Please, listen for a minute, listen to what I have to say," begs Monir. "I am not being unreasonable. I honestly can't tolerate being beaten anymore. We've been married a year. The beatings started from the first week. You're my parent. You could get the divorce thing going. I swear to God and the Prophet, he is crazy. What if he hurts me permanently, or kills me? What're you going to do then?"

Father lifts his head. His eyes are red, moist with tears. He lifts his hand and gently strokes Monir's hair.

"I know, dear child," he says, his voice quivering. "I know it is hard. But divorce is not a solution. People will talk. So-and-so's daughter is divorced. It is a stigma. It is bad for the family name. Just be patient for a while. God willing, things will improve."

There is a momentary silence. Father continues, his voice calm and tinged with authority, "Now get you going, child. Rasool has called to say he is coming to get you tonight. Pack your stuff and get ready."

THE DRIFTING PUFF of clouds has now left the darkening night sky. Father, Big Brother, and Rasool Agha are in the parlor. Monir is squatting on the floor of the living room across the hall folding her clothes and putting them in the sack.

"What're you doing, Monir?" I ask, as I gently touch her tear-soaked face. "You're thinking of going back?" Her eyes are hollow and expressionless.

"Are you going back?" I ask again. "Is that why you're packing?"

With the tip of an index finger she wipes a tear off the corner of an eye. "I've made up my mind," she says drily. She then turns toward the wall, leaning her head against it as she tucks her knees under her. She places her hands protectively to the sides of her head.

"Look," she says in a muffled voice. "When he beats me, if I fall to the floor against the wall with my hands on my head like this, it won't hurt as much."

ZOHREH HAKIMI is a short story writer and novelist. Her short story in this volume was first published in the Iranian feminist journal *Zanan*.

Grammar

Sofia Mahmudi

THE FUTURE IS NOT easily manipulated. It is capricious, and unwilling to conform to forecasts and predictions. It is prone to upset even the best-laid plans and reasonable aspirations. It can even alter the course of life and derail projects developed over a lifetime.

The concept that the auxiliary verb "will" in conjugating a verb in the future tense dictates the sequence of events implied by the main verb is a mere illusion. My own circumstance this morning is a case in point: I *will* go to school; I *will* take the grammar test; I *will* return home.

But the future may have other plans for us regardless of our will. Until this morning I was a person, a male adolescent named Asghar. Grammatically, I was a *concrete noun* because I had material existence detectable by the senses; I could be seen, heard, touched, smelled, and even tasted.

I was a *singular noun, a boy,* because I represented a single specimen of my species. I was identified by a *proper noun,* Asghar, which distinguished me from other adolescents within the periphery of my acquaintance.

What I have said so far has been in the *past tense*, when I was waiting anxiously to go to school, take the grammar test, and get it over with. But the future had different plans for me: a traffic accident, as I was crossing a busy street on the way to school, necessitated my transfer to the hospital and to the graveyard shortly thereafter.

Now I have grammatical designations different from the ones I had before the accident. I am now an *abstract noun* in the minds of those who knew me, because I am not a material being any more, but a spirit, an abstraction. I am no longer referred to as a singular noun, *a boy*. I am now among *the dead*, a *collective noun*. I have also lost my status as a proper noun, Asghar. I have now become a common noun modified by an adjective, "*poor kid*," a nomenclature referring to the countless unfortunate children in this world.

I have concluded that the definition of the "future tense" in grammar is not quite valid. Supposedly, it indicates an action taking place in the future:

"I will go to school for the grammar test."

"My father will go to the store for cigarettes."

Instead, I ended up in the hereafter world and my father in prison because, "The coroner's report, based on eyewitness testimony and the outcome of the autopsy, has determined strangulation as the cause of death of the party injured in the accident, the perpetrator being the father of the said injured party, who proceeded with the crime as the victim was being transported to the hospital, allegedly motivated by the prospect of financial gain as part of the coverage provided by the insurance policy held by the driver of the vehicle involved in the accident."

Those *simple* sentences in straightforward *active voice*, denoting my intention to go to school and my father's plan to go to the store, through the failure of the *future tense* to perform its function, were transformed into a murky *complex sentence* made dimmer by a string of verbs in *passive voice*.

SOFIA MAHMUDI is the author of two short story collections, The Woman and Her Child with a Sparrow and a Song and Jumbled Words Puzzle, which was a result of her work at a center for runaway girls in Tehran. She studied sociology and Russian, has translated several works from Russian and English into Persian, and works as a teacher and librarian.

Dogs and Humans

Fereshteh Molavi

IT WAS A SOUND that tore me out of the nightmare—a new sound, a small sound. The light behind the frosted windowpane has grown faint. Heavy, wounded eyelids! The sound of the abandoned puppy. How soon she deserted him! Two or three times, at dawn and at dusk, I have seen the female dog. During the day, she is cautious and keeps her distance—not a look, not a sound. Still, she is uneasy. She prowls around the ruins, disappears behind a tree, takes shelter behind a wall. A helpless sound. Was it Youssef calling me from the bottom of the well? The hand that has reached out in vain drops down. The puppy, unaware of the female dog's anxieties, wanders along the side of the alley. Will he stay?

Behind the door to his room, I hesitate. I rest my hands on the doorframe. Hollow legs. From behind the window of that room, or from behind the door to this room? From wherever it came, it was a sound that was beckoning me. Without a response, the mouth remains closed. The front door opens. "Dad, don't forget your promise," Youssef calls out.

"No, I'll buy you a toy today. Bye!"

Just this. The front door closes. So, he has been awake and has not called for me. Why did I fall asleep? A carefree female dog? I don't think I heard a shot being fired! I swing the door open. The morning's smiling mask. The faint light has obscured the moonlit face. Old voices echo: "Pay attention, you shouldn't be checked in chess game so quickly and so often!"

"But I still haven't been checkmated."

"You haven't? When you're checked, you will be checkmated, too."

The constant check. The sword overhead shakes only slightly—not to fall, but so that it won't be forgotten. The smooth forehead is coated with sweat.

"Why didn't you wake me up?" I ask.

A small dove is perched on the window's edge.

"Is it hurting again?" I ask.

The dove doesn't move.

"Are you feeling hot?"

The dove flies away. He frowns.

"Do you want me to open the window?" I ask.

He turns away and irritably says, "You ask so many questions, Mom!"

I go to the kitchen. I prepare his breakfast. I set the tray next to his bed.

"How long do I have to stay like this?" he asks.

"Until you get better."

"What if I don't get better? What then?"

I don't answer him.

"Huh?" he asks again.

The tedious, repetitive smiling mask. I say, "If Grandmother was here, she would say bite your tongue and don't be a naysayer! She's supposed to come and stay with you today."

I wipe the sweat off his forehead with a tissue.

"So, you're going to work today?" he asks. "Can you not go?"

"My leave is over. But if it becomes necessary, I'll take more days off."

He hands me the half-empty tea glass. "You mean if I don't get well."

I open the window and gently say, "Be patient!"

"Until when?" he snaps back.

"Until the doctors figure out why your leg hurts."

He clenches his fists. "I will not go to the hospital or to the lab again."

"So you don't want to get up and walk again?"

"My leg hurts really bad when I put my foot down on the floor. You're not the one in pain . . ."

I'm not the one in pain? Grandmother arrives. The stairs have made her breathless. She rubs the palms of her hands on her aching knees. I pour some tea for her.

"I've come so that you can go to work," she says. "Just tell me what medication he has to take and when."

I put on my coverall. "For now he doesn't have to take anything. His fever broke. If it starts again, he should take a sedative. He knows which one it is. And for lunch . . ."

"I know! Get going!"

I take my handbag. I kiss Youssef's damp hair. "Call me if there's anything."

His gaze is fixed on the dove perched on the tree outside the window.

"Did you hear what I said?" I ask quietly.

He turns and murmurs, "Don't make it fly away again."

I tiptoe out of the room. I open the front door. Grandmother calls me.

"When did he come back?" she asks.

Puzzled, I reply, "Who?"

Youssef says out loud, "Grandmother, she forgot her headscarf again, didn't she?"

So the dove has flown off again. I yank at the corner of the black headscarf hanging on the clothes rack.

The road is long and the sky cloudy, but along the edge of the ruins a ribbon of green has sprouted. I see neither the female dog, nor her puppy. Young boys are lying in ambush behind the brickworks—with empty hands, without rocks and sticks and slingshots. Their stare follows me all the way to the corner of the alley. Cats and crows are prowling around the heap of garbage bags—our city, our home. Which slogan has made dogs the bane of the world? But there was no sound of a shot being fired last night! Not always, once in a while, at night the sound of dogs barking engulfs the alley. The night shatters. Finally, a hand dials the telephone number and at dawn the sound of the city services' car breaks the silence. The wheels come to a stop. The click of a trigger and the sound of a shot . . . then . . . a howl and a moan. So when will all of this end? You release your breath out of your chest. You open your eyes. You see the faint sign of dawn through the hazy windowpane. You close your eyes again. You bury your face in the pillow and push away the blurred image of the puppy who is ignorant of the decree of execution. Can you not hear a new sound?

Old voices echo: "So there's always a puppy left behind."

"Not to live, but so that the sacred providence is achieved."

"Perhaps this is a manifestation of the Satyagraha philosophy."

"Is the female dog rejecting fate when it breeds?"

"When Adam was eating the forbidden fruit, he was giving in to fate."

"Sin is secondary. What is primary is the ordained punishment, which is concealed by the superfluities of what is secondary. The door to the hell in which Raskolnikov was burning will not open with the death of the old woman."

"Then perhaps sometimes sin only shows us the way to purgatory . . ."

"Was there moonlight on the night the woman left home and headed for the ruins or the temple?"

"That night is all I remember from Pearl Buck's *The Mother*. Now I can't remember if the woman considered doing this to be a sin or not."

". . . and, for instance, if that old woman had the same fate as Job, wouldn't she have considered Raskolnikov to be her savior?"

"But if Raskolnikov commits a great sin, and hoping for salvation prefers certain anguish to the torment of uncertainty, then the Chinese mother, confused by the unwarranted punishment, resorts to sin."

"When retribution is the decisive justification, being guilty is equal to being innocent. K. must be put on trial; and the principle outcome of a trial is punishment. That's all."

"So in the beginning there was just punishment and . . . sin came later when . . ."

Illusions are muddled, the road is long and the day gloomy . . . when my Youssef can still find joy in seeing a small fearful dove, then why can't I hear the sounds of spring?

At the bus stop, I sit on the bench next to a bulky woman wearing a black chador. I pull my black headscarf further down on my forehead. A heavy drop falls on it. I look up. The crow sitting on the awning, which has a hole in it, doesn't budge. I look down. I take a crumpled tissue out of my black coverall's pocket. The woman in a black chador watches me with her mouth open. I turn away. Now and then, Grandmother says, "None of God's actions are without wisdom, even his wrath . . ."

Old voices echo:

"It is thus that there's wisdom in items and objects, as well . . . for instance, in Pahlavi brief shorts . . ."

"But why are they called 'Pahlavi'?"

"There must be a wisdom to this, too. It seems that other than loose pants, the Qajars didn't have any other clothing to cover their privates . . ."

". . . the poor woman is flustered and stammering. Well, when from the crack of dawn, before she even opens her eyes, in addition to cooking and cleaning and sewing and the kids' homework, she also has to worry about shopping and the race for coupons and the length and width of all sorts of lines, she can't be carefree."

"The woman next door brings her news of the government distributing cooking oil. She knows that if she doesn't hurry she'll be cheated out of her share. And as she grabs her toddler and rushes out to go to the cooperative, she forgets to cover her hair."

"Well, the street was empty and the few passersby didn't have the energy or the patience to order others to abide by the law, and one can't expect anything from a toddler who has just started to talk."

"Near the bazaar, when she catches sight of the patrol car, and even then thanks to people's signs and gestures, she suddenly realizes that . . ."

"Her shopping bag was plastic, not cloth."

"She sees the child's Pahlavi shorts at the bottom of the bag . . ."

"No way! She pulls it off of the kid."

"She can't think of anything to do other than to pull the shorts over her head."

"Of course . . . and when she escapes danger by a hair and a tragic story becomes a hilarious one, it sets her thinking about the benefits of the shorts."

"Now if the shorts weren't Pahlavi shorts and instead had legs, wouldn't the patrols have grabbed her?"

"I agree that an insignificant pair of Pahlavi shorts can ward off disaster, but what is the wisdom behind the can of fuel and the box of matches that in the middle of the street burn both the veil and the veiled?"

"It's obvious. They not only set a desperate woman free, but they help the snitches and stoolies get their hands on a scrumptious meal."

"May God save us from this sharp tongue that even when held captive won't stop stinging."

The bulky woman gets up and shakes her black chador. The bus approaches. The crow hasn't moved from its place. A cat, having received his morning's ration from the nearby butcher's shop, saunters over and leaps up onto the bench. I stand up. The bus stops—men enter from the front door, women from the middle door. The woman holds onto the bar and moves to the left. There isn't room to move in the women's section. I go to the right. The seats are all taken, but not a single man is standing. A few young girls wearing full head covers and a woman carrying a child climb on board behind me. The bus sets off. The crow screams and leaps down next to the cat lazing on the bench—peaceful coexistence. Wasn't the decree banning dogs from life introduced to parliament by cats and crows? The girls are holding the edge of their head covers as shields and they're whispering and giggling. The woman holding a child, who is also carrying a heavy duffle bag, staggers with every jolt of the bus and grumbles in response to the child's nagging. At the next stop, a man gets up from an aisle seat. Overjoyed, the woman flops down into it. The man sitting next to her gives her a sideways glance and pulls himself away. One of the girls who is clutching a binder and a few books mumbles, "The poor thing, his boundaries have been violated!" Her bangs are jet black and she has subtly lined her large eyes with kohl. The girl next to her, who has blond bangs and light eyes, swallows her laughter and says, "Then he should go back to where he came from." A third girl says, "As a matter of fact, they've designed the buses this way to cut back on the cost of women traveling." The bus stops. In the men's section, a man gets up from an aisle seat on the driver's side and gets off. The girl with the black bangs looks around, sits down, and puts her binder and books on her lap. The man next to her is a young Afghan. He doesn't take his eyes off of the crowded street. Now there isn't room to move in the men's section either. I look the other way. Among the women I see the bulky woman in a black chador. She is seated. I reach for the window to open it, but it's so filthy that I don't have the stomach to touch it. I pull back my hand. How many more stops until we reach the circle? The woman holding a child gets off. A young man takes her seat. There is fighting and commotion at the front of the bus. The driver stands up and shouts, "Come on, move to the back! I can't drive like this . . ." The standing passengers reluctantly move back. The driver catches sight of the girl with black bangs. He raises his voice even louder. "Get up! Are you dense, sitting wherever you feel like it? I'll be suspended for ten days . . ." I collect myself even more to make some room for the girl with black bangs. Is Joseph's Well more confined than a female dog's grave? But it seems there was no sound of shots being fired last night! I peek around among the coveralls and headscarves. I press the bell. The girls are neither talking nor laughing. At the bus stop, I struggle to make my way through the crowd and hop off.

At the edge of the circle, I remember the time. The people waiting for taxis are restless. Some uselessly run after those that drive by slowly, others feign ignorance and move a few steps ahead of the person who had arrived there before them. A few, frustrated by their wrong assumptions about which taxi will stop, retreat a few steps, others will not even refrain from jabbing and kicking . . . I pull my sleeve back as far as is permissible to reveal the watch strapped tightly around my wrist. My attendance card will be marked in red now. Grandmother will be angry if she finds out I'm late. She believes my tardiness will make the halal morsel I earn to become *haram*. When Youssef looks at her quizzically, she holds her tongue as long as she can and when her little boy's curiosity piques, she gravely explains, "You see, my son, all that is wrong in the world is because of this mixing up of *halal* and *haram* . . ." A passerby treads on my foot.

Halal and *haram* aside, Grandmother loves to talk. Was I wrong to tell her Youssef had had enough of her chattiness? But the dove shouldn't stay silent when . . .

A dilapidated taxi pulls up in front of me. A few people climb out. A male passenger remains in the backseat. I open the front passenger door and climb in next to the driver. I eye him furtively. He doesn't have a beard. I mumble, "Straight ahead." He doesn't ask how far. I sigh with relief. Perhaps I will reach my destination before the taxi becomes too crowded. It makes no difference whether the passenger in the back is fat or thin. Regardless, men usually sit sprawled out. And if you end up sitting in the middle . . . God forbid if the passenger next to you decides to pour out all that he has kept bottled up inside! The taxi stops. A stout man carrying a briefcase gets in. The taxi drives off. Right before the intersection, the driver slams on the brakes. Ignoring his curses, the pedestrian who has jumped in the middle of the street walks away. My gaze falls on the corner of the side mirror and the wide grin on the face of the stout man with the briefcase. I look down.

There is a postcard with a picture of cats on it taped to the dashboard. The driver brakes. Two men run toward the taxi. The driver turns to me, casts his eyes down and says, "Lady, I'm sorry, but you need to go sit in the back." I don't move from my place. The two men reach the taxi. More quietly, the driver says, "Just yesterday, I was fined . . ." I open my handbag, put my fare in his hand, and climb out of the car.

Slowly and quietly, I walk past the reading room. The librarian is napping at the circulation desk—the price of spending the night taking on passengers to earn a little extra driving them around. I don't feel like exchanging pleasantries. With my head down, I walk past the stack room. I open the door to my office. My colleague and office-mate, holding the telephone receiver, half rises from her chair. She can't bring herself to wrap up her conversation. "A daily report of the son-in-law's actions to the mother-in-law." This is what the librarian at the circulation desk repeats every day at around noon, when she is no longer sleepy and stops by the office behind the stack room. I run my fingertip on the corner of the desk to check for dust. My colleague and office-mate smirks and shrugs. The tissue box is empty. I close the desk drawer and wipe my finger on the corner of my headscarf. I go through the books piled up on my desk. My colleague and office-mate covers the receiver's mouthpiece and whispers, "You came back before the end of your leave?" I nod and smile—the usual smiling mask of the morning. The janitor walks in with a dust cloth. She is still wearing black . . . but these days black is no longer a sign of being in mourning. I open the small window behind me and turn my chair around so that I face the shaded lawn. The janitor asks about my Youssef. What can I say about her Ismael? My colleague and office-mate hangs up the telephone. When she's done with her pleasantries with me, she tells the janitor, "You didn't show up yesterday. There's dust everywhere!" In a choked up voice the janitor replies, "I went to the cemetery." My colleague and office-mate picks up a book and walks out. I doubt my memory. I ask, "Did they turn him over to you?" The deformed fingers rub the dust cloth aggressively over the desk. "You know what his father is like," she says. "Even if they turned Ismael over and he buried him, he wouldn't allow me . . ." The tired hand stops moving. I point to the stool in front of the cabinet. She sits down and leans her head against the edge of the cabinet. I turn away. Doesn't the shade fall on this corner of the lawn? My colleague and office-mate returns. I hear the squeaking of her chair. She turns on her transistor radio. She can't forgo listening to the Home and Family program. Of the economics courses she took during her undergraduate studies, she claims to only remember Charles Fourier's theory of work: jobs should be assigned based on the worker's interests. A crow is wandering around in the middle of the lawn. I turn my chair. The janitor solemnly gets up and resumes her work. The host of the radio program is interviewing the mother of a martyr. My colleague and office-mate turns up the volume. "Even if I had ten sons, I would willingly and with a clear conscience send them all to the front . . . we are content with the saints' and prophets' approval . . . we yearn for heaven . . ." The telephone rings. The deformed fingers fold. My colleague and office-mate turns down the volume on the radio. I pull a large book in front of me and flip through it. Among the stories about the prophets, I find the story of Ibrahim and his Ismael. They give Ismael to Ibrahim, then demand his sacrifice and again forgive him to Ibrahim! I close the book that makes no mention of Hajar. My colleague and office-mate hangs up the telephone, and carrying a book, heads for the stack room. I swing my chair around. The tranquil crow finds it impossible to tear itself away from the lawn. "When was I ever a mother to my Ismael!" the janitor says. "After he was born, my husband threw me out of the house empty-handed . . . All these years, I tolerated being apart from my Ismael, hoping that once he finished his military service he would come to me . . ." The tired hand drops down. The deformed fingers claw at the side of the coverall. "And yesterday?" I ask. She looks up. A faint smile appears on the corner of her mouth. "I visit strangers' graves. It makes no difference, does it?" I stand up. I take my handbag and head home.

AT SUNSET, the cloud that made the day hazy turns into rain. Is there no end to Ya'qub's tears? Youssef's chapped lips move.

"The dove will definitely get wet."

I close the window and say, "It will find shelter . . . perhaps . . . shall I close the curtain?"

He restlessly shakes his head. I drop my hand.

"What was happening outside?" he asks.

"Nothing."

He looks at me skeptically. "Is that why you came back so early?"

I put the pitcher of water next to him. "I shouldn't have gone."

He raises his head from the pillow. "You said your leave had ended."

I don't look at him. "I won't go anywhere again until you've recovered."

"Why?" he asks, confused.

"If you take your medication, your pain will ease and your fever will stop."

He puts the pill on his tongue. I hand him the glass of water. He swallows the pill and the water. "You're tired of illness," he says. "Just like he who comes home late."

I lay his head back on the pillow. "He will come and he will bring you a toy."

I sit on the edge of his bed.

"I don't want a toy anymore," he says irritably.

I run my hand over his tousled hair. "It will do you good to sleep. I will tell you the story of Youssef . . ."

ARE THEY GOING to kill the female dog, but spare the puppy? A new sound, a small sound. Eyelids wounded by light close in the darkness. The blast of the bullets being fired tears the darkness into shreds. They throw my Youssef in the well for the sin of being loved. In the end, who is going to interpret my sleep and my wakefulness? In the empty and silent reading room the shelves tremble and the dusty books shake. My colleague and office-mate sneezes nonstop and dials. How many zeros are there in the telephone number for City Hall? Does the female dog abandon the puppy and go to the ruins on a moonlit night? Grandmother always says disaster follows sin. Youssef looks at her with disbelief. The sword hanging overhead is always shaking. No one puts cats and crows on trial. K. must be punished; so should the taxi driver who doesn't tape a picture of crows on the dashboard. But Raskolnikov is searching for earthly punishment. Is that the sound of the front door? But Youssef doesn't want a toy anymore. The janitor takes the rag out of her uniform pocket. Hajar disappears in the dust of the old book. Grandmother says no stranger's grave will be the same as Ismael's. Does Ya'qub cry over his own heartbreak or over Youssef's shirt? All the clouds in the sky descend to darken the earth. Will the flames from fuel and sulfur drive away the darkness? Grandmother bites the skin between her thumb and index finger and says, "Of all impossible things! How could a pair of Pahlavi shorts properly cover the privates!" The girl who has lined her eyes with kohl holds her binder in front of her bangs. A fire that can be extinguished will not replace the sun. The rain at dusk drenches the dove. Grandmother says they finally pull Youssef out of the well and return Ismael to Ibrahim and . . . but the rain that blurs the earth and sky will not bestow on Ya'qub even a sliver of sun the size of the palm of a hand.

They come and take the puppy away. The female dog remains. She remains? The hand that was vainly reaching out drops down. The absent sound, the closed mouth. I lift my head off the covered sheet over Youssef's legs. The female dog rejects fate. Doesn't she?

Born in Tehran, **FERESHTEH MOLAVI** has written many novels, essays, and short story collections, including *The House of Cloud and the Wind*, *The Departures of Seasons*, *Dogs and Humans*. She moved to Canada in 1998, and is a member of PEN Canada.

The Queue

Shiva Arastouie

SHE DECIDED AGAINST the jeans. Instead, she pulled out a pair of black, loose-fitting pants from the drawer and put them on. It had been seven years since she had worn those loose black trousers outside. She had always pushed them aside every time she rummaged in the drawer choosing something else to wear. Her jeans, on the other hand, hung on the closet door ready to put on whenever she went out shopping.

She had only two coverall uniforms. She took the darker one off the hanger and put it on before starting to look for her black Islamic headdress, something that would cover her hair and neck draping over her shoulders. She hadn't worn it for seven years and couldn't remember where it was, so she decided to wear a scarf and fasten it under her chin with a safety pin. She was reminded of her husband, who in situations like this would say, "Darling, just knot it under your chin and relax."

She changed her mind, started looking for the head-dress, and finally found it at the bottom of a box of old clothes. Pulling it on her head, she felt some satisfaction in its discovery.

She then checked her handbag to make sure she hadn't missed anything. Seven years ago she carried a much larger bag, almost the size of a briefcase, the one she had left at her mother's.

"These days," her mother would say, "girls carry a suitcase over their shoulders when they go out in the streets."

She used to pack her handbag with all kinds of stuff, from books and stationery to hairbrushes, lotions, a mirror, painkillers, adhesive tape, sterile gauze, cough suppressant, nail files, thread and needles, stockings, hair clips, deodorant spray, and sanitary napkins.

"Naturally," her mother would say with a touch of sarcasm, "if you're going to be out and about all day, you need all this stuff."

She remembered her black binder, and now had to look for it in the pile of old books and notepads to retrieve the university ID card inserted in the pocket on its front cover. She pulled out the perforated card and placed it in her small handbag, which could hardly accommodate anything else other than her wallet, eyeglasses, and key ring.

She had taken the last examination seven years ago. The hall monitor had punched a hole in the corner of her ID card, as confirmation of her presence in the final exam, and returned it to her. She thought of the day she had her picture taken for the card. She had worn the black headdress and had wiped all traces of makeup off her face. "Try not to frown, Miss," the photographer had advised. "Think of happy things." She had thought of her admission to the university and the picture had turned out satisfactorily. She looked fresh and youthful. Even the official in charge of issuing student ID cards commented on it positively, as he affixed it to the card and stamped it in the corner. She looked at the back of the card and was pleased with the data: age 24, female, hazel eyes, brown hair, weight: 54 kilograms, height: 162 centimeters, and blood type: O negative.

There was no comment under "Restrictions," only an ominous "Warning" declaring: "Any attempt to forge, alter, or abuse this card is an offense subject to prosecution."

The only alteration to the card since then was the punched hole in its corner, which gave it an added air of authenticity. The picture on the card lacked the prescription glasses, which she would now need to locate Room 374, the office where she was supposed to go, according to the announcement in the newspaper, to get her suspended degree. The glasses were now on the table in the hallway, a space which also served as a living room as well as a reception area when they had guests or visits from their parents. She had left them on the table the night before, going to bed after turning off the television. One side faced upward and the other, attached to the frame by superglue, was slightly askew. When she wore them, they did not fit securely behind her ears. She thought she should have them in her handbag to look for the room numbers.

Next, she looked at the footwear lined up at the bedroom door. They were all summer-season sandals and open-toe shoes. The problem was that they had to be worn with thick socks —and she hated the feel of them on her feet. In earlier days she always wore boots or shoes that covered her feet up to the ankles so she didn't have to wear socks regardless of the season. In conversations with other women on clothes, shoes, and other matters of fashion, she would say, "It is as if I breathe with my feet. Every time I put on socks or stockings I feel strange, like someone is choking me. I have to take them off to breathe."

Some women would have the same feeling, "Yes, yes! Me too!"

Other would roll their eyes and say, "Oh, really!"

It took her a while to make up her mind to breathe or not to through her feet. Ultimately she decided to breathe through her nose, which happened to be naturally shapely and well-formed. Women often asked, "Where did you have it done? It looks so nice."

"It is my own, I swear to God!"

"Oh, really!"

The problem was that she didn't have any socks. She thought of borrowing a pair from the landlady. After all, she had loaned the woman a basket of potatoes—which she hadn't yet returned. She felt she could ask her for a pair of socks.

Her feet, clad in black socks, fit snugly in the white sandals, although the color clash made her cringe and avert her eyes when she looked herself over in the hall mirror. Other than the absence of the big handbag and black binder, she didn't look any different than seven years ago.

The night before, she had placed the binder on the hall table and thumbed through its pages to see if she remembered any of its contents after seven years.

She reached for the house key in the door to drop it in her handbag. But she then decided to leave without it, surely her mother and daughter would be home to let her in. She had persuaded her mother to come over and stay with the child for the day so she could attend to her business. Her mother had shown some reluctance, what with all the broad beans she had to clean and store for winter. She had offered to help and her mother had consented.

Wearing a thick pair of black socks, an overcoat, and her headdress, she stepped out, ready to face the outside world. Seven years was about the length of time since she had walked the streets on her own, now she couldn't make up her mind whether to catch a cab or take the bus. Most of her outings were limited to shopping for staples in the neighborhood or taking her daughter to the nearby school. Her husband bought the newspapers and magazines on his way to work. In the past seven years she hadn't had any reason to think about public transportation. On Fridays, her husband's beige-colored Renault, as if programmed, would take them to their in-laws and bring them back home at night. It even seemed to know which set of in-laws to visit each alternate Friday. On the way back, her daughter would fall sleep on her lap. Sometimes she herself dozed off after the car traversed the bridge.

"Last night we were watching videos at my mother-in-law's until past eleven," she would report to a friend over the phone. "It was an old movie. My husband loves old movies. We asked if we could borrow the video, but they said no."

"Oh, really!"

But better than any movies, she liked to watch the windows of the houses alongside the bridge. At night, when they were crossing the bridge, she would put on her spectacles and peer through each window as her husband drove past them. There was something in each window that made it different from others. Before they got to the bridge on their Friday outings, she hardly looked out the windows of the car. Nevertheless she knew every moment where they were. She was not interested in the clothing stores, which she found boring. But she was fascinated by green grocers and fruit stalls. She had to suppress an urge to make her husband stop the car to buy fresh fruits and vegetables in large quantities. She didn't like bakeries and confectioner's shops either, especially the silly conical hats they supplied with birthday cakes. Their daughter always insisted on them for her birthdays and her husband always obliged. She always made sure she wore one for her birthday photograph. By now they had seven of those hats at home. She had made up her mind to leave them behind in case they had to move.

Anyway, most shops were closed on Fridays, but the windows of houses were always there. Even if the lights were out in some of them, she could imagine what was going on inside. With or without people behind the windows, she had a sense of the atmosphere that permeated the darkened spaces. If the lights were out, it meant that dishes had been washed and were drying in the strainer, or that they hadn't yet been brought back from the dinner table. She would catch glimpses of men in pajama bottoms and women with their hair in buns behind their heads, just standing there. Before she could see what they were doing, the car would pass the window. It was like thumbing rapidly through a photo album. Just the attempt to guess the nature of the human interactions through a fleeting glimpse of the people seen in the window excited her. After they crossed the bridge, she would close her eyes and reflect on the succession of impressions she had seen through those windows.

Some windows revealed living rooms. She was struck with the uniformity in their furnishings. The windows were treated with delicate, transparent sheers. A sofa and matching armchairs were arranged around an oblong coffee table over which hung a chandelier of modest size. There was always something of ornamental nature in the middle of the coffee table—a crystal vase, an artificial flower arrangement, or an antique china bowl, she guessed. Every room had a large framed tableau or print on the wall directly above the sofa. Again, she could only guess what they depicted: a bunch of multicolored flowers in a bowl with some blooms strewn around it, or a stormy seascape with a schooner in the foreground leaning at a precarious angle, or a woman with long, wavy tresses seated on a highly ornate armchair. Or it could be the same tableau she had over the sofa in her own living room, representing a country house in a snowstorm. Once she had thought of taking it off the wall altogether, but she found that without it the room looked strangely bare and uninviting. Without it, she felt out of place watching TV, reading newspapers, helping her daughter with homework, cleaning vegetables for dinner, sipping on a cup of tea, or even dialing a number on the phone. In due course, the picture went back on the wall.

Along the bridge, there was one window she found more intriguing than others. It opened to a fairly large kitchen with metal cabinetry painted lime green and a dinette set in the middle. An old woman, always wearing a cardigan, regardless of season, would be sitting on chair knitting. She was always in the kitchen whether they were on their way to or from their in-laws'. Sometimes she was on her customary chair and knitting; she might be looking for something in the cabinets, or cooking something over the stove, or just moving aimlessly around the kitchen.

If she was not actually knitting, the skeins and needles would be still be visible in a heap on the table.

In some windows at various times she could see young girls in different outfits and hairdos talking to someone not readily visible. In other windows she saw adolescent boys leaning out of the window surveying the traffic on the bridge.

All in all, crossing the bridge, especially at night, was a pleasant experience. The good thing was that the bridge had a long span, and her husband, sensing that she enjoyed her pastime, drove more slowly when they crossed it. Now she was on her own and wondered in what way her impressions would be affected if she crossed the bridge in a taxi or on a bus.

AFTER SOME HESITATION, she decided to take a cab. Everything had changed since then; using the buses required a skill that she had lost after seven years. In those days, she knew all the routes and bus numbers, and managed her commute so that she could do some studying and preparation on the bus. There were some passengers so regular that their presence or absence would tell her if she was late or early. On the bus she would scrutinize the faces of the passengers or make a note of what they read. Sometimes, when she had nothing to read or prepare for class, she would steal glances at what the passenger next to her was reading. Most passengers resented this practice. They would either close their books or reposition themselves so she wouldn't be able to see what they were reading.

"How dumb! So what if I know what they read?" she would think to herself.

Sometimes a passenger would write a phone number on the margin of his reading material and tip it over so she could see it.

"How vain! He thinks I am in love with him!"

She would then turn her head away and divert her eyes to other passengers until the bus arrived at the campus, her destination.

The campus was crowded with faces and people, although in class she had to keep her gaze on her instructor's face—which she subjected to a series of assessments: If the nose were a little less prominent . . . His eyes are too closely set and his hairline recedes too far . . . His lips are too thin, clashing with his bushy eyebrows . . . He must have had a better complexion as a young man . . . concluding with a complex hypothetical exchange of facial features involving professors of literature, linguistics, philology, literary translation, and deconstructive theory. If all this could be done, then everything would be fine.

Even at her wedding she got bored looking at her own face next to the groom's reflected in the mirror as the cleric recited the marriage vows. She felt better after the ceremony when a lot more people and faces showed up for the reception. At the end of the night, after everybody had left and the lights had been turned off, she had a lot of faces in her mind to keep her busy till morning.

Now that she got into the cab, she positioned herself in the backseat so as to be able to see her face in the rear-view mirror. She was pleased that her eyes, eyebrows, nose, and mouth looked good together and individually, although her face could not be considered strikingly beautiful and could stand some improvement by makeup.

She thought of what lay ahead: she would present her punched ID card to the official in charge, as per instructions in the newspaper, and finally receive her degree, which had been languishing in the Ministry of Higher Education because her field of study had been suspended. On the way back she would buy some dill weed and, once home, using the broad beans her mother had bought, she would prepare a delicious rice dish and offer it to the family ceremoniously as "my graduation banquet!"

To reward herself for her efforts, she would stay in bed until noon the next day. In three days it would be Friday, when they would drive across the bridge.

At the entrance to the building she produced the ID card from her handbag and showed it to the security guard before putting on her glasses. She saw a long line of women already formed on one side of the long corridor. She took her place at the end of it. An equally long line of men stretched on the other side, and a young man joined it almost at the same time as she joined the women's. She looked at her wrist to see what time it was and found that she had left her watch at home. She would be out of there by noon, at maximum, she thought. Soon she started feeling bored. To amuse herself she looked probingly at the faces of the women ahead of her in the line.

It occurred to her that looks had generally improved since seven years ago. She took off her glasses and put them back in the handbag. She wouldn't need them until she got to Room 374. Besides, that was where everybody was going. But there was no movement in the line. She thought of analyzing faces again as a diversion. So she put the glasses back on and surveyed the crowd, and noticed that it was becoming thicker by the minute. Both lines for women and men had almost doubled in length since her arrival. A familiar face caught her eye. It was the man who had come at the same time as she. He was at the same position in the men's line as she was in women's. "It doesn't matter what I look like," she thought to herself. "He's probably already married and has children."

By now, her boredom had intensified and an incipient headache was setting in. She thought of getting some fruit juice to drink. She looked at the three or four women ahead and behind her in the line and tried to memorize what they looked like. Two of them were positively good-looking, and a couple looked too young to have graduated seven years previously. She caught snatches of their conversation.

"Three hundred dollars a month. Indian Embassy."

"Better than being cooped up at home."

"My husband doesn't want me to work. We don't need the money anyway."

"No, I'm not married. I do some translation at home."

"We started a translation bureau—with some classmates. Instead of bachelors we got associate degrees."

"We opened up a fitness gym."

"I went to England and took a cosmetics course. Pays better than translation."

"Oh, yes. I saw your article in the paper. It was interesting."

She turned to the woman in front of her wearing heavy makeup and asked her to save her place in the line, "I have a terrible headache. I'm going to get something to drink and be right back. Thanks a lot." The woman nodded reassuringly.

She put the glasses back in her handbag and headed for the exit. She remembered a juice bar at the top of the street she and her classmates used to frequent in the old days. It was still there. She ordered a glass of carrot juice and drank it slowly. When she returned to take her place in the line she was astounded to see that the lines had now extended out of the building and to the corner of the street. People were rushing from all sides to join them. There was no more space for parking and the cacophony of car horns was deafening. She hastened to enter the building.

"Hey, lady. End of the line!" the people shouted as if in a chorus.

"But I have been inside, I swear. I just got out to get . . ."

Her plea was drowned in shouts of protest.

Nevertheless, she pushed her way past the guard into the building. Ignoring the screams of objection from the crowd inside the foyer, she found the two women before and after her in the line. The makeup seemed to have been washed away from the face of the women in front. They both looked pale and seemed to ignore her. When she tried to take her place between them, they started yelling at her.

"Outside! End of the line!"

This seemed to galvanize everybody in the line. They started repeating the injunction like a refrain in a chorus.

The situation was threatening. She felt everyone staring at her and retreated to the exit and went back to the street. By now the lines had gone around the block and half-way down the next street. People, both men and women, were rushing to join their respective lines. Shopkeepers were closing their shops and taxi drivers and bus conductors were actually abandoning their vehicles and hurrying to stand in the line. She had no choice but to go back to the end of the line. To distract herself from her predicament, she began examining faces in the crowd, imagining them with different noses, eyes, and lips. She noticed that slowly but perceptively color was draining from all faces. She felt the headache returning, but she knew she should not leave the line to seek relief. She put on her glasses to see faces farther away, hoping to take her mind off her headache. But looking at the sea of faces stretching interminably intensified her headache, and standing in line for hours made her feel nauseous. She thought she would vomit if she did not leave the line. She looked at the woman in front of her, the one whose aquiline nose she had replaced with a more delicately shaped nose of another woman with unplucked eyebrows.

"Do you also have a headache?" the woman asked her.

"Headache and nausea," she replied. "I'm about to throw up."

"Try the park around the corner," the woman suggested. "Come back soon, so I can go too. OK with you?"

"Yes. Sure," she said enthusiastically. "Great idea!"

She found her way through the crowds to the next street, which was totally deserted. In the park she drank from the fountain and splashed some water on her face. She slumped on a bench nearby and closed her eyes. She started feeling better.

The same thing happened once she tried to get back to her place in line. There were heated objections and offensive remarks as she walked up the street toward her position. The woman looked paler than before and her nose seemed longer and more pointed.

"What are you talking about?" said the woman. "I don't remember you. My head is bursting, too. You shouldn't have left your place."

"Go back to the end of the line," another woman yelled at her.

"Why are you shouting?" she objected. "Oh, my head!"

By now the din was overpowering and in the stifling atmosphere she began drifting toward the end of the line around the block. Her headache was better, but she could not see where the line ended. She wished she had tolerated the headache like everyone else and had not left her spot. She had lost track of the time, didn't know how long it would take to the get to the end of the line. Tired and dispirited, she felt dizzy and disoriented, and the line seem to be moving in an undulating way. She had lost track of time as she closed her eyes trying to concentrate. When she felt somewhat steadier, she opened her eyes and found herself in front of a door in the office foyer—now eerily deserted and quiet. Hurriedly, she put on her glasses to check the number above the door. She was elated to see 374. As she opened the door to enter, a man blocked her way.

"Time is up until further notice," he said.

"Oh, for God's sake," she implored, "please let me in. I am the only one left."

"Sister! you are not the last one in line," said the man. "Many people gave up and left before you. Come back for the next round."

"Next round?" she exclaimed. "When is that going to be?"

"We'll announce it in the papers," said the man coldly, as he closed the door.

It was already dark when she left the building. The streets were deserted and there were no cabs or buses to be found.

She felt exhausted and powerless. "How can I get home?" she wondered. Her mother and daughter would be worried. Her husband would be back from the office waiting for her. A taxi service was up the street, she recalled from the old days, although she had never used it. But she couldn't find it anymore.

A car rounded the corner and stopped before her. The driver beckoned her to get in. Hesitantly, she slid in the backseat. The driver was looking at her in the rearview mirror. "What are you doing in the streets this time of night?" he asked.

"I came to retrieve my university degree," she answered involuntarily.

"Oh, yes. I got mine some time ago," he said. "It is getting too late, but don't worry. I'll take you home. I know your address."

She leaned forward to take a look at him. His profile seemed vaguely familiar. It no longer matters what I look like, she thought to herself.

"How do you know my address?" she inquired.

"I was in love with you once," he declared. She sat bolt upright and motionless. She could not come up with anything to say. She held tight to the back of the front seat, at a loss for words.

"Once I came to your house to tell you that," he said, passively. "You weren't home. I said I was a classmate and wanted to speak to you. They gave me your new address. But I didn't try it. I knew it was too late."

"Oh, for goodness' sake!" she finally blurted.

The car stopped in front of the house, and she got out fast, muttering "Thank you" under her breath. The car drove away.

She stood in front of the door wishing she had the house key. What if they were all out looking for her? What if everyone had given up on her and gone to bed? She really wished she had a key to get in.

She rang the bell and waited. There was no response. She rang a second time. A window was open and the curtains pushed aside. She realized there was a blackout. That explained the prevailing darkness in the neighborhood. She pushed her face against the screen on the window and noticed that there were lights, perhaps oil lamps, burning in other parts of the house. Through the window in dimmed light, she saw her daughter seated on the floor in the middle of the room cleaning vegetables. She tried to say something but could not make a sound. Incapable of uttering anything, she peered through the screen again and noticed her old black binder on the table with a conical birthday hat on top and several others scattered around it. She chuckled silently. Internally, she felt an urge to say something or call someone, but still she could not make any sound. She put on her glasses and looked around for more details and noticed that the framed picture over the couch had been replaced. She stared at it intently and recognized her own likeness. It seemed to be one of her old pictures that had been enlarged to poster size to fit the frame. She was wearing an open-neck dress with her wavy hair falling over her shoulders and was seated on an ornate armchair. She didn't remember ever taking a picture in that pose. Her nose in the picture seemed to be altered. Reflexively, she touched her own, trying unsuccessfully to say something.

WITHOUT KNOWING WHY, she glanced down at her feet and noticed the thick, black socks. She bent down slowly and took them off. Reinserting her bare feet in the sandals, she could easily breathe. She looked again through the screen at the figure of the young girl sitting on the floor cleaning a pile of greens, which she recognized as dill weed. Intuitively, she knew that was her daughter and felt a longing for her and her touch, but was unable to get her attention. From across the hall she could now see part of the kitchen. The cabinets had been replaced with metal ones painted lime green. She saw her mother in a cardigan seated at the dinner table knitting. She felt a heartwarming sensation at the sight, although still felt a knot in her throat making her incapable of speaking. She noticed her jeans hanging from the coat rack in the corner of the hall, and the old pair of pants the young girl was wearing as she casually handled the pile of greens in front of her.

Now exhausted and dispirited, she slid down the wall and squatted on the pavement. She returned her glasses to the handbag and took out the ID card. She moved slowly to the front door and banged on it with her fists. There was no response. She slid the card through a crack in the door and returned to her place under the window. She looked across the street as she sat there against the wall. What she saw was a bridge being crossed by cars moving at high speed in both directions. There was no sign of cabs or buses. She noticed a beige Renault crossing the bridge more slowly than other cars.

She heard the telephone ring and the voice of her daughter say, "No, mother has not yet returned."

SHIVA ARASTOUIE is the author of several works in both prose and poetry, including the short story collection, *Came to have Tea with my Daughter*. She was born in Tehran, and is a creative writing teacher at the College of Art in Tehran.

Tehran

Moniru Ravanipour

IS THIS THE SAME avenue once called Mossadegh?[1] And what are these department stores, with such elaborately designed windows and red-carpeted floors. Are they the same shops you used to run past like a flash of light in early dawn, with stack of leaflets under your arm, to slip them under their closed doors?

Was it on this same spot that you and other demonstrators would cry out, "Bakhtyar[2] the Chattel! No Better than Cattle!"

Or was it in front of this store where you heard another group of demonstrators shouting "Wrap the Shah in His Shroud! Make Our Country Proud"? And you haven't forgotten this intersection where you stood with your raised clenched fist shouting "Hundred Percent Bani-

[1] The historic tree-lined Pahlavi Avenue was renamed after the 1979 revolution in honor of secular, democratically elected prime minister Mossadegh, but with shifting political fortune, it is now called Vali Asr, a reference to the twelfth Shia Imam.
[2] Shapour Bakhtyar (1914–1991), the last prime minister of the Shah's regime. He was murdered in Paris by the elements of the current rulers of Iran.

Sadr,"[3] and here pressed against the wall, you watched with excitement the waves of demonstrators marching down the street.

Wave after wave has passed and now here you are standing in front of a furniture store window full of luxury merchandise. Go ahead. Look as much as you want. They have charm and elegance worth looking at. No one, I mean not one single person, recognizes you on this street anymore.

The sales clerk, courteous, well-trained, and well-dressed, approaches you. "Welcome!" he says.

You must smile at him by way of acknowledgment and cast a sweeping glance over the inventory, as if you are making a choice. You must pretend you are a buyer and not a loafer, wandering in memories of bygone days. You point to a dining set with six chairs.

"This set. How much?" you ask.

"Three million tomans."

You must appear to be unfazed. You pull up one of the chairs and sit on it, as if testing it for comfort.

"Not very comfortable," you announce.

"There is this other one," says the man as he points to a nearby set. "It costs more."

"Money is no object," you casually remark.

---

[3] Abolhassan Bani-Sadr (b. 1933), the first president of the Islamic Republic. He had a falling out with the dominant figures of the regime and was impeached in 1981. He had to skip the country to avoid execution. Currently he lives in exile in Europe.

You look the set over. It takes your breath away. But brown leather upholstery clashes with your kitchen counter, you tell the man.

A little lie never hurt anyone.

The man nods his understanding. "We'll have another consignment coming from Italy in a few days," he volunteers.

You get his card, turn around, and leave the store.

The next stop is not a jewelry store, though it is harder to get in. You have to ring a bell and wait to be buzzed in.

Now you can feast your eyes on vases, fine dinner plates, and the assortment of dishes tastefully displayed on shelves.

"This vase?"

"Two-hundred-fifty thousand tomans."

"This fruit bowl?"

"Seven-hundred thousand."

The fruit bowl is engraved with a portrait of Louis XV. It is hard to imagine that this is the same man who did not take baths from year to year, now depicted on this porcelain bowl resplendent in his royal garb holding a scroll in his right hand. You trace the image with your finger, as if to ascertain the verity of this historical tidbit.

"Please don't touch." You hear the attendant behind you. He is a good-looking young man with knotted brows and a serious mien. He seems to know full well you are not likely to make a purchase. No, you shouldn't touch the items on display. You can only point to them, point to Louis XV, whose body odor gave rise to the perfume industry in France.

You hear the young man clear his throat, suggesting that you should move on. So you get past the fruit bowl and stop to examine a long-stem crystal glass as if it's been made for Cleopatra's hands. This time you don't reach to touch the receptacle. There is no use pretending; the bewilderment in your face has already betrayed you. Your idle, flailing hands give away the inner anguish. So, you shove them in your empty pockets. Desolate eyes can be shut to all that is surrounding you, but hands, where can these forlorn, despondent hands find an abode?

YOU LEAVE the store, fearful lest you break something if you stay longer. You look at the solitary porcelain pedestal in the window. It reminds you of a ballerina standing on delicate, shapely legs.

No, this kind of luxury store was not here in those days. How long ago were "those days," anyway? When did these stores and these tower-like, high-rise buildings appear in this place, you wonder. And this small park? It was not here in those days, or was it?

You move slowly and awkwardly. The legs that carry you are not the twenty-year-old legs on which you flew from street to street, alley to alley in those days. They are fifty years old, laboriously carrying your bloated, barrel-like figure toward the little park with a playground, where children nimbly climb up and down the jungle gym.

In a few more steps you will arrive at a bench. But you are intercepted by a thin, shabbily dressed man. He is trying to say something, but what he utters are incoherent sounds. You have a feeling he is trying to compliment you, or your outfit. He joins his index finger and thumb as a congratulatory gesture, suggesting that you have hit the mark. He is pointing to your posture and the crimps of your skirt as if wordlessly telling you 'you are number one,' communicating his approval of the way you look.

Now the stores, the towers, the jungle gym, and the children recede to the background. All you see is the man's face; it looks young, and it is flushed. Is it because he is shy? You wonder. Do you remind him of someone—his mother, perhaps? But no son looks at his mother this way. There is a glint in his eyes as he looks you up and down and moves his hands in the air. How long has it been since the last time you blushed because someone looked at you this way? You can't read lips, but something tells you the sounds he makes indicate that you are the object of his admiration.

You look at the man and try to reciprocate by a smile. He is still looking at you approvingly. You are aware of a woman, young and attractive, sitting on the bench nearby. She is smiling at you. At you or your adventure?

"I don't know what he is trying to say," you address her, trying to sound exasperated by the encounter.

"Be careful, lady," she responds. "They're a gang."

"A gang?" you utter in disbelief.

She is wearing a pink silken headscarf that charmingly frames her attractive face. She shakes her head authoritatively.

"You see," she answers. "As one of them distracts you, another one snatches your purse."

You are loathe to believe it. The man is still standing there, but he makes no more gestures. He looks alarmed. The woman smiles, revealing a perfect set of white teeth.

"Look, take out your cell phone," she whispers, "and say you are calling 110,[4] Then watch what he does."

Involuntarily, you produce the cell phone from your handbag. Loudly enough for the man to hear, she says: "Call 110." The man turns around and walks toward the street.

The woman points to a motorcycle parked at the curb. "He's going to get on that cycle," she says. You watch as the man jumps on the motorcycle and speeds off.

You lean back on the bench. Now you are aware of the intense heat, traffic noise, and the screeching children on the jungle gym. Perspiration runs down your face. You slip the cell phone back in your handbag and take out a pack of cigarettes. And the lighter? There is no lighter.

"I'm a smoker, too," says the woman, "but I leave my cigarettes and lighters at home when I come here."

[4] The Iranian equivalent to 911 service in the United States.

You ask some passersby. They don't have lighters either.

"I'm sure you can find one in that little shop," the woman suggests.

The shop is at the end of the park. You must carry yourself on worn-out legs for fifty yards or more to get to it. Right there at the presence of male customers, you light your cigarette, indifferent to their gaze. Slowly you return to the woman on the bench and she welcomes you with a sweet smile. You feel at ease sitting next to her.

You draw heavily on the cigarette, and light another one with it after three or four puffs.

Weary of the noise, heavy traffic, and polluted air, you remark, "How everything has changed!"

"Things change almost every second," she says.

"In those days this street was filled with trees."

"There are no more trees left. It's all concrete, traffic," she says. "And all sorts of gangs," she adds, as an afterthought.

You cast a glance at the traffic-choked street and remember the days when it was crowded with pedestrians. You think that you are not like a barrel but a ladder, a ladder many used to climb up to luxury stores, to a sound and safe seat, and well-stocked bank accounts.

"Do you always smoke so much?" the woman asks, with a note of concern in her voice.

"Only when I think of the past," you answer.

"Memories?" She says. In her big, bright eyes you

notice a shimmering of tears. You are afraid they may flow down her cheeks.

"But you are not that old to remember those days."

"We all have memories of this town," she says, a touch of melancholy in her voice.

"But memories differ from person to person."

"That's right. I was a child during the bombardments,"[5] she says, staring into the distance.

"It wasn't only bombardment," you interject.

"Yes, I know," she concedes. "It was an internal battle. All that street fighting."

"One thing is sure—there was more security in those days," you assert. "We don't have that anymore."

"Yes!" she agrees emphatically. "For a while now I've stopped taking a handbag with me when I am out and about. I just carry my keys and cell phone in my pockets."

She then looks at the children playing in the park. Something like a spark glimmers in her eyes. "We must watch out for them especially," she says.

In a pleasantly soft voice, she recounts some stories she knows about this town: solitary women who have been assaulted and robbed, children who have been kidnapped, young people who have become drug addicts.

You are thirsty. Very thirsty. You wish you were floating in a pool of ice water for relief from this cursed heat

[5] A reference to the Iran-Iraq War (1980–1988).

burning up your body, your brain. You touch the woman on the shoulder.

"I'm so thirsty. What would you like to drink?"

She lifts her face to look at you. You notice her prominent cheek bones and long eyelashes almost touching her eyebrows.

"I shouldn't trouble you . . ." she says as she makes an attempt to rise. You respond with pressing down on her shoulder and walk toward the shop. Gradually, her soft voice, and her winsome smile replace the noises and the heavy traffic.

So the world isn't all ugliness and smog, you decide. It is still possible to sip on some refreshment with a stranger and enjoy her company.

She takes a sip from her drink with some relish. You ask, "Do you come here often?"

"As often as I can, usually early in the morning, while the air is still fresh," she answers.

Her cell phone rings. She produces it from her coat pocket and lifts it to her ear in one continuous, graceful motion.

"Hello? . . . Hello? . . . Hello? . . ." She speaks into the mouthpiece. "I got cut off," she tells you, shrugging her shoulders.

You feel an urge to ask for her phone number, chat with her over dinner at a small restaurant nearby.

"It hit the spot," she says, referring to the bottle of soda, which she places on the ground near the bench.

Her cell phone rings again. Again, she is unable to keep a connection. She turns to you smiling, disarmingly, alluringly.

"Do you live alone?" you ask, somewhat concerned that you may have been too nosy.

"Yes, if the gentlemen let me," she responds. You both laugh at the implications of the rejoinder.

You exchange addresses and phone numbers. You enter hers in your cell phone.

The beginning of a friendship, you tell yourself. This calls for a celebration with couple of sodas, later dinner in a restaurant, and then, who knows? Perhaps an invitation to her house?

You have been waiting for five minutes or so at the shop for your turn to get couple of sodas. Now you get the bottles and pay for them with the loose change in your pocket. From the distance you see no one on the bench. You hurry back, holding a bottle in each hand. You look around, hopefully, expectantly. No one in sight, no one.

You reach in your handbag for your cell phone to call her.

No cell phone.

No wallet.

No ID card.

You have been robbed.

MONIRU RAVANIPOUR is one of the most prominent writers of postrevolutionary Iran. She is the author of several distinguished novels, including *Heart of Steel*, *Gypsy by Fire*, and *The Drowned*. Her collections of short stories, *Kanizu* and *Satan's Stone*, were translated and published in the United States. A former Brown University fellow at the International Writers Project, Ravanipour now lives in Las Vegas and is affiliated with the Black Mountain Institute at the University of Nevada.

ACKNOWLEDGMENTS

I WOULD LIKE to thank the Feminist Press, and Gloria Jacobs, the former executive director of the press, as the sources of inspiration and support for this project. Special thanks to my friends in Iran, who helped collect many short stories for consideration in this volume. I am grateful to Faridoun Farrokh and Sara Khalili for their excellent translations, and the invaluable help and spirit of cooperation they brought to this project. My special thanks and gratitude to all of the writers in this collection. I am particularly grateful to Moniru Ravanipour for her excellent guidance on the translation of her short stories. I express my deepest gratitude and appreciation to all involved.

The Feminist Press promotes voices on the margins of dominant culture and publishes feminist works from around the world, inspiring personal transformation and social justice. We believe that books have the power to shift culture, and create a society free of violence, sexism, homophobia, racism, cis-supremacy, classism, sizeism, ableism, and other forms of dehumanization. Our books and programs engage, educate, and entertain.

See our complete list of books at
feministpress.org

THE FEMINIST PRESS
AT THE CITY UNIVERSITY OF NEW YORK
FEMINISTPRESS.ORG